CANDY HEARTS

A So Over the Holidays Novella

ERIN MCLELLAN

***Candy Hearts* (So Over the Holidays #2)**

"Erin McLellan delivers again with a sexy and sweet story, filled with humor, heart and hope, for your Valentine's Day reading pleasure."

—Layla Reyne, author of the bestselling Fog City Trilogy

"Erin McLellan's Candy Hearts *is perfect for your sweet tooth. Sexy, sensual and ever so slinky!"*

—L.J. Hayward, author of Death and the Devil Series

"Every book Erin McLellan writes is a sweet treat waiting to be unwrapped. Benji and William tick so many of my catnip boxes and kept me wanting more with every page."

—Allison Temple, author of the Seacroft Series

"Candy Hearts is blazing hot Valentine's fun that is jam packed with delightful tropes and sex toys. Exactly the level of heat I needed to melt the winter blues."

–Rachel Reid, author of the Game Changers Series

***Stocking Stuffers* (So Over the Holidays #1)**

"The sexual tension sizzled from start to finish. McLellan weaves sex toys, experimentation and curiosity perfectly into the intimate moments between Sasha and Perry … Get this book as a gift to yourself for the holidays!"

–Rachel Kramer Bussel, editor of Best Women's Erotica of the Year Series

"With a Scrooge-like heroine who owns her sexuality with a boldness that is admirable and refreshing, and a sensitive hero who's a lover of romance books and family, Stocking Stuffers is a fun, kinky and yes, swoony, holiday romance packed with laughs, hot sex, emotion and a love that will have you rooting for the happily ever after in ugly Christmas sweaters."

–Naima Simone, USA Today bestselling author

Mechanic Benji Holiday is so over Valentine's Day and men who don't get him. A weekend getaway with friends to escape the holiday hubbub is exactly what he needs. But William O'Dare—a stern and silent nightclub owner with "Be My Valentine" practically stamped on his forehead—throws a wrench into Benji's plans.

William has spent years focused on his career, and it has cost him friendships and love. Inexperienced in the business of romance, he's on the hunt for the perfect partner, and he's armed with specific criteria to guide him. But William didn't expect a hunky mechanic wrapped in satin and lace to show up on his doorstep.

Unable to resist their attraction, Benji and William agree to be secret fake valentines for the weekend, but secrets have a way of getting out. William gets struck by Cupid's arrow, and as the weekend winds down, he doesn't want fake or secret. He wants Benji to be his valentine for real and for keeps.

Candy Hearts is a male/male Valentine's Day novella featuring a house party power outage, meddling friends and siblings, naughty lingerie and naughtier toys, homemade Valentine's Day cards, and a happily ever after.

To the best lowkey valentine ever.

Chapter One

Everything was bleak. The icy, gray morning. The wind off the murky lake. The dark windows of the lake house.

Benji's love life.

And nothing was worse than having a bleak love life on Valentine's Day.

Benji stared up at the A-frame lake house through the windshield of his truck. There was one other vehicle here—a fucking Alfa Romeo, and damn did Benji hate working on Alfas—but the house looked deserted. None of the lights were on. There was supposed to be a hopping Valentine's Day party here. He pulled out his phone to check the email invite from his sister.

From: Sasha Holiday

To: Benji Holiday

Subject: V-Day Sucks Weekend House Party

Ready for your best V-Day ever? Join us, little bro. You deserve a Valentine's Day away from the bullshit. The whole gang will be staying at 40 Lakeshore Drive on Copper Lake. Get there anytime on Thursday after 10 A.M. House has a pink door.

Smell you later,
Sasha

Well, this house did have a tacky pink door, which Benji loved because he loved tacky things, not because he was excited about hanging out with the owner of an Alfa Romeo Giulia at an ugly lake.

Best V-Day ever. Not. Sasha had a habit of over-selling, but Benji had needed a weekend away, so he'd been willing to give this house party a chance.

You couldn't escape the disaster that was your singledom when everything about a holiday was created to remind you that life sucked when you were alone. Benji was over it. Over the dating scene. Over unsatisfying sex. Over the romantic-industrial complex called Valentine's Day.

Well, actually, he wasn't over it at all, but he was trying to be. He was trying very hard.

He grabbed his duffle bag from the seat beside him. It was stuffed with what he was lovingly calling his *Self-Love Boring Weekend with Sasha's Friends and New Fiancé* kit. He planned to spend the long weekend drinking, eating too much candy, and spoiling himself. He didn't need no man. He had a bag of pretty underthings and sex toys.

And those sex toys didn't cheat on him. Or wear crappy cologne. Or roll their eyes at his reality TV obsession. Or make him feel dumb and young and wrong.

He knocked on the candy-pink door. After a gazillion years, the door swung open and revealed a white man in flannel pajama pants, a ratty college sweatshirt, and intellectual-Daddy glasses.

They stared at each other. Benji had never seen this man in his life, which was odd. He thought he knew all of Sasha's friends.

Benji pinned him at thirty-five to forty years old. A streak of silvery white washed through the hair pushed back from his high forehead, very Cruella de Vil realness, but the rest of his hair was a rich brown and wavy. He had a dramatic nose—a high arch and a prominent bump —that lent his otherwise blandly handsome face some character. Plus, his tortoise-shell glasses made him look like a stern librarian wet dream.

"Who are you?" the guy asked.

"Uh. Hi!" Benji held out his hand to shake. "I'm Benji Holiday. I'm here for the anti-Valentine's Day weekend."

The guy frowned and didn't take Benji's hand, which was *embarrassing*. "The plans changed. No one was supposed to get here until tomorrow."

Heat flushed from the top of Benji's head down his face and neck. "Well, you're here." This was Sasha's fault.

"I own the house."

"Why did the plans change?"

"I don't have any power. They're doing scheduled

maintenance and updates to the substations in the area. It was publicized a few weeks ago out here, but I missed the memo since I live in the city most of the time. Didn't find out until last night. Did Sasha not tell you?"

"No. Shit. I shouldn't be here."

Bleak, bleak, bleak. Benji's body suddenly felt too awkward and too slow and too hot. But not like the *heyyyy* kind of hot. More like the he-could-definitely-smell-his-own-sweat kind of hot.

He closed his eyes and took a deep breath. His emotions were right on the surface. Had been for months, ever since his last breakup.

Damn, he wasn't in the mood for awkward small talk. He could have stayed home and done the club circuit with his friends. Gone to places named Splat and Verve and Blue. Or their newest fave—Mount. Bars with one-syllable names to show they were hip and fun. Hell, he could have contacted his ex for a booty call and the consequent tanking of his self-esteem. Actually, that was probably why Sasha had bullied him into coming—to prevent ill-advised ex sex. But all those options would have been better than the blank stare in front of him.

"Hey." The man's voice was gruff. "It's okay. Not the end of the world. Why don't you come inside?"

Benji followed the guy over the threshold. "I can drive back. I don't want to intrude."

"You just surprised me is all. Come in, and you can decide if you want to stay or not."

The inside of the house was dark and a bit nippy, but there was a blazing fire in a big brick fireplace and a kerosene lantern on the coffee table. It would have been cozy and romantic if not for the frigidness wafting off Benji's new friend.

"What's your name?" Benji asked.

The guy blinked a few times, his eyes sparking behind the thick frames of his glasses. "It's William O'Dare. I'm sorry. I want things to go according to plan, so I'm a bit … out of my element."

The crazy thing was, William O'Dare seemed perfectly *in* his element surrounded by the soft, warm light. He could have been a flannel-pajama model or in a commercial for something all-American, like Ford trucks or Old Navy or homoerotic contact sports.

William was older, hot, and stern—Benji's kryptonite. Though William was in casual clothes, he was commanding. Exactly the type of guy who usually made Benji feel ridiculous and silly. Exactly the type of guy he craved anyway.

"Plans are made to be thwarted," Benji said.

"Not my plans."

Well, this was a fun and enlightening conversation. Benji set his duffle bag down and scratched a hand through his hair.

"How do you know my sister?" he asked.

"We're friends."

Yeah, no shit. Talking to this man was like talking to a gorgeous wall.

Benji glanced around the room, trying to think of something to say. The house had a beautiful open plan interior with a modern kitchen and large windows overlooking the gloomy lake. He spotted a shuffle of papers on the coffee table next to the lantern.

"What are you working on?" Benji inched toward the table, hoping to catch a peek.

William sucked in a startled breath and gathered the papers before Benji could see, depositing them on the kitchen counter out of Benji's view.

He'd expected his Valentine's Day to suck. All that love in the air. Benji had figured it would hurt to be alone. Again. But at least at a house party he'd be alone *with other people*. The point was to be surrounded by Sasha's outrageous friends so he wouldn't have time to dwell on his overwhelming loneliness.

Then, when he was tired of being entertained by other people, he'd disappear to his room in this stranger's house and *entertain* himself.

"Will. Do you go by Will?"

"Not really."

"Okay. Cool." Yikes. This super sucked. "So, you seem uncomfortable, and I have no idea what the right move is here. Should I leave? I can leave."

"No. Stay. You drove three hours to get here. That is, if you don't mind no light or electricity. Or limited heat. The hot-water heater doesn't require electricity, but the furnace does, unfortunately."

"Should I just disappear into a room? Also, do I get my own room? I could probably keep myself occupied in there for a few hours."

"Doing what?"

A fierce tenor of emotion in William's voice made

Benji double-take. This was getting ridiculous. Benji wasn't going to tiptoe around this dude for an entire day. He'd rather spend three hours driving back to the city.

"Jerking off and eating Valentine's Day candy most likely. Unless you can think of a better option?"

William's mouth fell open and his gaze slid from Benji's face, down his neck and chest to his legs. *Whoops.*

"I didn't mean sex with you," Benji blurted. "That wasn't the option I was suggesting. I meant Canasta or adult coloring." Oh God, what if Benji had read that look totally wrong? "Not that you were going to offer sex. Fuck, you might not be queer. I'm sorry. I was kidding about jerking off." *Huge lie.* "But I do have candy." *Truth.* "I'll share. Not in a transactional-sex kind of way, but because candy is nice, and I'm good at sharing."

A sickening, gaping silence followed.

William's lips curled up slowly, and it was like the sun coming out from behind clouds. It was angels singing and trumpets blaring. It was unicorns and fucking rainbows. When frowning, William was handsome. That crooked smile made him burn-your-panties-off hot.

"Candy sounds great. And not in a transactional-sex kind of way. Also, I am queer."

"Oh, good."

Oh, good? Fuck, this was getting awkward.

Well, awkwarder.

"Yeah, good. Why don't I show you to your room?" William reached down and picked up Benji's duffle bag, chivalrous all of a sudden, which appealed to Benji in a weird, deep-seated way.

He followed William up two flights of stairs to an attic bedroom. He wasn't thrilled by the unplanned exercise—climbing stairs was for suckers—but watching William's butt in those flannel pajama bottoms as he took each step made the hike worth it. Benji wished he could get a better read on him. William was either a still-water-runs-deep guy or boring as fuck.

"Figured I'd give you the best room—first dibs, you know? Is that okay? You're the only one on this floor. Plus, it has the wood stove to keep you warm tonight."

"That's fine."

The room had a sharply sloped cedar-plank ceiling, a decadent bed covered in pillows, a wood-burning stove in one corner, and an en suite bathroom. But the best feature was the floor-to-ceiling windows and glass sliding door covering the entire A-shaped wall. The door led to a small balcony. Light filtered in through the wall of glass, brightening the room. The frozen water in the middle of the lake was visible, darkening as it melted close to the shoreline.

A room with a view.

This was a freaking master suite.

"How many bedrooms are there?"

"Four. I mean, five."

"Wow. That's a lot."

William shrugged, almost self-conscious, which was silly. If Benji owned a weird house with a pink door on an ugly lake, he'd flaunt the fuck out of it.

"Where's your room?" Benji asked next.

"It's on the ground floor off the kitchen. The other

three are on the second floor. Anyway, I'll get out of your hair while you settle in." William dropped the duffle bag, and it thumped loudly when it hit the ground, making them both jump. "What's in that thing?"

Benji swallowed hard. "Sex toys and lingerie, mostly."

____

Chapter Two

*S*ex *toys and lingerie.* The words crash-landed in William's brain. His tongue was too big for his mouth.

"Cool. Later," he mumbled, shutting the door and safely putting a bit of distance between him and Benji Holiday.

His lips were all tingly, and his ears were hot. Was this a stroke? Was he old enough to have a stroke? He'd smell toast if it was a stroke, right?

He'd felt like he'd been hit on the head with a cast-iron skillet when he'd opened the front door to reveal Benji on the porch. Benji with his acres of muscles, his pretty-boy face, his lack of brain-to-mouth filter, and his overalls.

William found him undeniably appealing.

But he was absolutely blowing it. He was normally totally in control, perfectly put together, completely composed.

And now he was in pajamas, for God's sake!

He jogged down the stairs and straight into his office to change into regular clothes only to be pulled up short by the pitch-blackness of the room. There was one tiny window, and it was covered by a heavy curtain. He fumbled his phone out and used some of its precious battery to turn on the flashlight.

While he was getting dressed, he heard Benji come down the stairs, so William rushed back into the kitchen to grab the dating criteria he'd been filling out when Benji had appeared. He hadn't been anticipating an interruption to his patheticness. William had had nothing better to do, stranded here alone with no power. Originally, he'd been planning to get work done—the Post-Valentine's Day Bachelorian Auction at Mount wasn't going to organize itself—but his computer had no charge.

His New Year's resolution this year had been to give this romance thing a genuine shot. In the past several years he hadn't had the emotional bandwidth to nurture a relationship and a burgeoning career. It hadn't been fair to other people to try. So he hadn't tried, living instead on the occasional hookup with acquaintances. His friendships had suffered too. He wouldn't be the owner of three successful nightclubs if he hadn't made compromises. His biggest compromise had been his social life.

But his career wasn't floundering any longer. He was doing well for himself and didn't feel the ache of wanting more, more, more. He was finally at a point where he could slow down, and rolling into his thirty-fifth year of life seemed as good a time as any. Too bad every date he'd gone on in the last month had been a circus and a half.

His best friend, Wren, had suggested thinking long and hard about what William wanted in a partner, to pinpoint the type of person who would mesh well with him—it certainly hadn't been Wren when they'd been together. William had always excelled at homework, so he'd created a list of criteria for his perfect partner using a template from the back of a self-help relationship book from the library. The template wasn't unlike the consumer profiles he and his business partner, Tina, made before opening a new bar or planning a big event.

But the last thing William wanted was for the bright and bubbly Benji to find all his hopes and dreams scrawled on a piece of copy paper.

He had just scooped up his dating profile and library book when Benji rounded the corner.

"Oh, you're dressed," Benji said.

William glanced down at his chinos and button-down. "Disappointed?"

"A little. You don't have to get dressed on my account. Hell, I was thinking of joining you. In pajamas. Not joining you in getting undressed."

Benji blushed, and William gobbled the man up with his eyes.

The wild, dark-blond hair. The wide mouth and freckled nose. The long, long legs and broad chest. His impressive height and huge hands. The overalls.

"Nice overalls," William said, his voice coming out a bit ragged.

Benji grinned. William couldn't stare at that smile for too long. It was like gazing at the sun. Something was blooming inside him, and intellectually he knew it was lust, but damn.

He skimmed the dating criteria in his hand, phrases jumping out.

Thirty-five or older

Business professional or business owner with high investment in career

Must enjoy nonfiction, The New Yorker, *and true-crime podcasts*

At the moment, his criteria felt like a pipedream, and it wasn't what he *wanted.* Not with Benji Holiday right in front of him wearing a tight white T-shirt, denim overalls, and a smile. William wanted to see Benji kneeling on the rug in front of the fireplace. He wanted to reveal all Benji's secrets.

That was probably not a good idea.

Was it?

No.

Well, maybe.

No, it definitely wasn't.

William turned on his heel, strode into his office, and deposited his dating criteria onto the futon. He probably had ten years on Benji. He needed to get control of himself.

When he returned, seconds later, he croaked, "Lunch?" They had limited food options, what with the power out, and he'd expected to be alone, so he hadn't gone to the grocery store. "I have the stuff for peanut butter sandwiches, and I put drinks in a cooler on the deck."

"I ate on the way, but I'd take a drink. Whatcha got?"

"Let me show you." William led Benji to the deck by taking him through the sunroom, which was a glassed-in room full of wicker furniture. William had planned to sleep out there on an air mattress once everyone else arrived.

The porch had a door that opened onto a large deck. The deck led to a short boardwalk that transitioned into a private dock. When William had bought the place, he'd imagined himself sitting out on that dock with his feet in the water, drinking up the sunshine, but he rarely made the trek out of the city to enjoy this place. He hadn't truly settled into any of the rooms except the office. And if that wasn't sad, William didn't know what was.

"Wow. This could be so pretty," Benji said.

"Could be?" William said, a laugh escaping. It was a lake. What wasn't pretty about a lake?

"Yeah, I mean, the water just looks cold and muddy. Is it prettier in the summer?"

It was true that Copper Lake wasn't exactly a tourist destination. That was one of the appeals to William. Property out here wasn't in high demand despite the waterfront. It was simply a muddy fishing lake, partially iced over at the moment, and surrounded by willows and scrubby grass. It had its fair share of snakes and catfish, but William had fallen in love with it the minute he'd seen the murky water lapping at the shore. He'd thought he could feel at home here one day.

"Yeah. It's pretty," he said.

In the summer, fishermen took rowboats out in the morning for their catch of the day, and the water smelled fresh and clean and, yeah, muddy. Cattails and lily pads covered the shallows, and toads sang into the night. It was beautiful in an earthy, unassuming way in the summer, but William also loved the starkness in the winter. The bare trees, the golden grass, the grey water.

Benji snorted and rummaged through the cooler, coming up with a can of local ginger beer. When he straightened, he said, "I get the impression you only say half of what you're thinking. As if you're actually waxing poetic in your head, but out loud you say, '*Uh, yeah, it's pretty*,' like a very gorgeous caveman."

"You think I'm gorgeous?"

"You own a mirror, don't you, caveman?" Benji walked back inside.

William had been called a lot of things in his life. Caveman was not one of them. Cavemen didn't wear Tom Ford dress shirts during a power outage, did they?

William looked down at his sleeve. Shit, maybe they did.

He followed Benji back inside and headed to the kitchen to make himself a sandwich. The house was open concept so he could see Benji arranging himself on the wooly rug near the hearth.

"What do you do for a living, Mr. O'Dare?" Benji asked as William slapped some peanut butter onto a piece of bread.

Guilt and shame bubbled up in William. Benji probably knew that stuff about his sisters' other friends. William had known both of Benji's sisters—Sasha and Rosie—for nigh on a decade, but he'd been notoriously absent for most of that time too. Too busy to show up to the big events. Too busy to be there when they needed him. Their annual Valentine's Day House Party was the only time he'd seen Sasha in years.

"I co-own a nightclub management business."

"That's fancy."

"It's mostly spreadsheets. What do you do?"

"I'm a mechanic. I specialize in imports and restoration."

William blinked a few times. He had not been expecting that. He wondered if there was grease under the fingernails of Benji's expressive hands or the scent of oil on his skin.

William took a bite of his sandwich so he didn't blurt out how much he wanted to stick his face in the join of Benji's neck and shoulder. Benji transferred his attention to the fire, which gave William a bit of breathing room.

After finishing his sandwich, William pulled a book off the shelf and moved to the chair closest to the fireplace. And Benji. Benji seemed content to sit in silence, and because William's intense and instantaneous attraction to Benji was muddling his brain, silence was probably good.

This sucked. Awkward silences sucked. Benji didn't really

do silence. He pulled his phone out. This was all Sasha's fault, and she needed to answer for her crimes.

He texted her: *What the hell?! Why didn't you tell me the party was postponed?*

He could tell she'd seen his message, but she didn't respond.

"That jerk left me on *read*," Benji said out loud after a few minutes, sort of talking to William but mostly talking to himself.

William was reading, but Benji hadn't seen him turn the page once. Anytime Benji glanced at William, William seemed to be staring at him.

"Maybe she's busy," William said, reasonably.

Benji hated reason. He glared at William and called Sasha.

"Benji," Sasha said. She sounded out of breath. "Where are you?"

"I'm at Copper Lake," Benji said slowly and with a lot of exaggeration. "Where are you?"

"Uh-oh."

"Yeah. Uh-oh."

She stifled a laugh, but it still came through loud and clear. "I decided to go into work today. I forgot to call you."

"I'd say, sis."

William placed his book face down in his lap and openly stared at Benji. That was worse than the surreptitious staring, but it also heated Benji's skin inexplicably. He should probably head upstairs to have this phone call, but he liked William's eyes on him.

"I'm so, so sorry," Sasha said. "I totally blanked and forgot to tell you the party was postponed. Then we got a shipment of beta tests in today, so the office was full of a possible new line of butt plugs. It was very distracting."

"Yeah, a shipment of butt plugs is not a good enough excuse, Sasha."

William jumped and knocked his book to the ground. Benji grinned. This was getting fun.

Sasha laughed. "I really am sorry. I'm the worst. You're the best. I suck. You're great. Do you forgive me?"

"Verdict's still out. So what's the plan? Can you come tonight?"

She hesitated. Never a great sign. "After William told us about the power outage, I told Perry's sister that we'd be there for dinner tonight. I don't want to bail on her. I have to impress the soon-to-be in-law."

Benji rolled his eyes. "Perry's sister loves you already."

"When is the power coming back on?" she asked.

He asked William, "When will you have power again?"

"Is he sitting right there?" Sasha asked, surprised. "Did he hear you say *butt plugs*?"

Benji ignored her.

"The electric company said it'd be back on by late morning tomorrow, but to call to verify," William said. He picked his book up.

"Tomorrow morning," Benji said to Sasha.

"We'll get there tomorrow afternoon at the latest. I think that's everyone else's plan too. If you drove back home tonight, you could ride with us tomorrow. Or you could just stay until we get there. I'm sure William doesn't mind."

"He said I could stay."

"You can." William's words echoed in the dark living room.

"See. Stay tonight and everyone else will be there tomorrow, and we'll have so much fun," Sasha said.

"Fine," Benji said. "But you owe me."

"Deal. I'll bring you something cool."

"Sweet." Presents from Sasha were either incredibly thoughtful or raunchy as fuck.

"Is everything okay there with William?" Sasha dropped her voice to a whisper, as if someone else could hear her. "He's super serious."

She said that like "serious" was the worst kind of offense.

"Yeah, it's fine." Benji grinned sharply at William. "But he's a total bore. He's reading."

"Well, I'll be there tomorrow. Are you going to be warm enough? Do you have food?"

"I'll be okay. Promise." Benji loved both of his sisters, but being the baby of the family came with baggage. Especially in their family. That was what happened when your parents were a shit show. Your sisters took over. "Bring me my present tomorrow."

He decided demanding presents was also part of being the baby of the family.

"Fine, you brat. See you tomorrow." Sasha hung up on him.

"I'm a total bore, huh?" William said, an insanely hot smile on his face.

Benji almost swallowed his tongue. "This was supposed to be a party. I came to get my mind off my utter aloneness, but instead, the universe has conspired to magnify it."

"You're not alone. I'm here."

Benji waved that comment away. "You know what I mean. The romantic ambiance is wasted on us."

William made a surprised noise in the back of his throat. After a few seconds, he said, "Why are you alone, then? You're young and hot and nice. I'd think you'd have partners forming a line."

"Sexual partners, maybe. It's a bit harder to get them to stick around."

"Yeah. I hear you," William said softly.

Benji narrowed his eyes. "Are we dishing about our sucky love lives? Because I might need some wine for that."

"Did you bring wine?" William asked.

"No. Do you not have any?"

"Unfortunately not. I was not in charge of food or drinks this weekend."

"Well, that blows. What are you smiling about?" Benji asked.

William schooled his expression, and Benji could have mourned. "Nothing. You're very intriguing."

"Are you making fun of me?"

William sat forward in his chair. "Of course not. I think I could listen to you talk for hours. Even if it's complaining about your love life. Even if it's complaining about being stuck here with me."

"That sounds boring too."

"What do you suggest we do, then?" William asked.

"It's your house." Benji said this petulantly, but with a small, ornery smile. He wanted to goad William into a reaction.

"I have cards." Benji brightened at that, then William said, "If you want to play Solitaire."

Benji laughed.

William continued, "You're welcome to my nonfiction. I own Doris Kearns Goodwin's entire catalog. There might be a book of Sudoku in my office."

"So you're not going to entertain me. Is that the message?"

A charged silence vibrated between them for one breath. Then two. Three.

"Oh, sweetheart, I'd do more than entertain you. If you'd let me."

Chapter Three

Benji froze. The pet name rushed through him. He loved that shit. Loved to be spoiled, to have sweetness dripped over him like hot fudge. Benji's sisters claimed he had a compliment kink, which was true, but not a fact he freely admitted.

It made him feel silly to ask for it. It was much better when it happened naturally, when someone just figured it out and fed him nice words and dirty sex in equal measure.

Not that William was offering him dirty sex, exactly. In fact, Benji wasn't sure what was going on. He could normally tell when he was being hit on, but things with William had been weird since Benji had arrived.

"Are you hitting on me?" Benji asked. It was better to get it all out in the open.

"Would you be okay with it if I were?"

"Yeah. Probably."

Hell, William was fucking gorgeous. And rich. And kind of silently sexy (or maybe boring—the jury was still out). He seemed to be loosening up, at least. So why not fuck? They evidently had a full day alone before anyone else showed up, and Benji's cell phone battery was not going to last that long unless he asked William if he could charge it in his car. Benji's old truck didn't have that capability. Sex was as good a way to pass the time as any other activity.

Now, *that* was definitely the attitude that had gotten him in trouble in the past, but William wasn't a Grindr hookup. *He owned property.* Surely that meant something. Benji hadn't slept with a property owner in ages. Or ever. People his age couldn't afford property. Thanks a lot, baby boomers. Or maybe that was the gig economy's fault? Benji was bad at current events.

But Benji was *good* at talking himself into bad decisions. The best at it, really.

William scooted forward in his chair, suddenly intent and focused on nothing but Benji's face. The low light in the room cast shadows over William's body, making him look harsh and deliciously wicked.

"What exactly do you want, Benji?"

"I don't know," he said.

"I think you do."

An idea popped into Benji's head as if it had been placed there by Cupid himself. He imagined pulling one of those arrows with a plunger on the end off his chest.

"I have the best idea."

"What is it?"

"So you know how Valentine's Day sucks? Especially when you're lonely as shit. And I am."

"Okay." William frowned.

That was not ideal. Benji wanted that unicorn smile back. He needed to lawyer the hell out of this proposition.

"I'm single. Are you single?"

William nodded. "I wouldn't hit on you otherwise."

Benji waved that comment away. He'd had plenty of non-single dudes hit on him. "Well, we're all alone for a while. It's Valentine's Day in two days."

"Okay."

"I've never had a valentine. Want to be mine?"

William blinked a few times, his face blank.

Mayday. Mayday. Big mistake. Big, even for Benji.

"Fake valentines," Benji said, in addendum.

"Why do you want to be fake valentines?" William asked, his face still scary neutral.

Well, Benji had been hoping for a "hell yes, let's bang," so this was super humiliating.

"Because! You're hot, and it'll be fun. We can be romantic and flirty without the pressure. Or, as romantic as is possible during a power outage in the middle of nowhere."

Benji had never had a valentine. And yes, Sasha had invited him to this weird Valentine's Day house party so he'd feel better about being single. This idea spit in the face of that, but Benji liked spitting in the face of things.

"Fake valentines," William repeated, nodding slowly.

"Yes!" Benji raised his hands in the air and pretended to have a *Rocky* moment.

William laughed. "What will being valentines with you entail?"

"Blowjobs?"

William's face registered half a second of shock. "Oh. Okay. Hello. So we're doing this."

Benji should have led with the blowjobs. He grinned and slid to his hands and knees. Then he unzipped William's pants and spread the fly open. Benji loved being on his knees. He loved the simultaneous feelings of power and supplication it elicited.

Yep, this was probably a bad idea. He didn't even know this guy, but he was so hot. And Benji was so bored.

He needed a keeper.

"Uh, oh fuck," William said as Benji leaned forward to nuzzle the impressive bulge in front of his face. "Umm. Wait, hnngh—oh." He loved that he'd reduced William to single syllables. Benji sat back on his heels, and William cupped his cheek. "We should have a safety conversation."

Benji pushed his face against William's hand. The heat from William's body washed over him, which was nice. The room wasn't exactly warm. If Benji was going to take his clothes off, he'd need to soak up all William's hotness, his heat, his attention.

"I had a check-up a month ago," Benji said. "Negatives across the board, but I've had sex since—hand stuff and gave someone a blowjob. I always use condoms for anal, and I'm on PrEP."

"Everything was fine at my last appointment, and I haven't been with anyone since then. Since way before then, actually."

"When was that?"

William's mouth went strained and tight on the edges. "The appointment? Nine months ago."

Benji gaped. "Nine. Months."

"Yeah. I'm busy."

"Oh, I'm gonna take such great care of you."

William slid his fingers down Benji's cheek and gripped his chin. "Will you be vocal with me?"

"Kinda hard to be vocal when my mouth's full of your dick." Benji wasn't the most emotive in bed. He tried to do exactly what his partners wanted, tried to be perfect for them. Which meant he was usually too in his head, too inauthentic. Too scripted.

That—changing himself to appease shitty men—was his whole fucking problem in a nutshell. Maybe he had daddy issues. Or mommy issues. Parental issues? He had Issues. Capital *I*.

"Just be honest," William said. "You don't have to fake-moan or anything. I want to know if you enjoy what we're doing. If you don't. Where your head's at."

"Yeah, okay."

William combed his fingers through Benji's hair. "So gorgeous on your knees for me. I've been imagining you right there on that rug, kneeling, since you got here. You like being there?"

Benji melted at the touch. "Uh-huh."

He finally allowed himself to get a good eyeful of

William. He was wearing tighty-whities, which shouldn't have been hot—Benji was a bit of an underwear enthusiast, so he had *opinions*—but they were. The fabric clung to William's erection and contrasted starkly with his dark treasure trail. Benji followed a path up the inside of William's leg until his nose nudged William's balls.

"That's it. Pull it out." William's voice was gentle and his eyes assessing, as if he couldn't tell if Benji would enjoy taking orders.

Benji *so did*.

He slipped the underwear down William's legs, helped along by William arching off the seat of the chair for him. He had an amazing fucking cock. Fat, long, and uncut with a prominent head peeking from the foreskin. It was shiny at the tip, wet already.

"Take it. Please," William whispered.

Benji kissed his way up the underside of William's cock until he reached the loose sheath around the head. A bright salty tang burst on his tongue, mixing with the meaty, musky taste of William's skin. Benji pulled on the foreskin lightly with his lips.

"Oh, Benji. You like being a little cocktease, huh?"

The words sent a shudder through Benji.

William's pulse was a visible drumbeat in his throat, his lips parted, his eyes hooded and fixed on Benji.

"I like you staring at me as if you want to see through my clothes," Benji said.

"I do. Take your shirt off. Wanna see your chest."

Benji's hands trembled as he unhooked the braces of

the overalls. He let the bib fall to his waist and started to lift his T-shirt over his head.

Then the reality of what he was about to do hit him. Hard.

It hit him that he was wearing a baby-pink harness and lacy jockstrap under his overalls. Oh fuck.

He'd never … never done this.

Well, he'd given blowjobs, of course, but he hadn't revealed this part of himself—the part that wore pretty underthings on the regular—to a sexual partner. He'd tried to broach the topic with his ex, but it hadn't gone well. At all. There had been laughter involved.

"You don't have to take your shirt off," William said. "We can stop." William was watching him too intently, reading all kinds of things in Benji's hesitation.

"I don't want to stop. But …"

"Whatever it is, you can tell me. I'm your fake valentine, remember?"

Benji closed his eyes and tried to weigh his options. One of his newfound goals was being open. Being himself. Not changing who he was while in a relationship to satisfy someone else. So maybe this would be a good start. It wasn't real, which made it safe. William had promised to be a good valentine. This was practice. For both of them.

And if it went poorly, Benji could leave. No harm, no foul.

Right?

Benji whipped his T-shirt off.

William gasped, the sound almost drowned out by the logs crackling in the fireplace.

"What do we have here?" William ran a shaky fingertip over the strap at Benji's shoulder. "I thought you were kidding about the sex toys and lingerie."

"Wasn't."

"Yeah, I see that. Damn, you firecracker. Fuck."

When Benji had put the harness on earlier, he hadn't expected anyone to see it. He simply enjoyed feeling the straps and silk and lace on his skin. He'd needed an extra boost of confidence, and having something sexy on under his clothes, like his own inside joke, helped him get his butt in gear.

The straps of this harness were pink and butter soft. It was one of his most expensive pieces. He'd gotten it after going to an adult-novelty convention with Sasha. She was a dildo slinger (okay, she was the head of marketing) for a sex toy and lingerie company called Lady Robin's Intimate Implements. The harness had cost half his paycheck.

Worth it though, to see the dumbstruck expression on William's face as he fingered the delicate straps. His breath was coming out in shuddery gusts, and his dark eyes were wide and hungry.

So hungry.

"Oh fuck," William whispered. "I, uh. I'm not … God. I've never seen anything like you."

"Do you like it?"

William nodded. "Like *you*. Like *you* in it. Do you wear this stuff a lot?"

"Yes. Kind of." *Just never during sex*, Benji almost said, but he realized he was skirting way too close to something he'd secretly wanted for as long as he could remember. He didn't want to jinx it or have to explain it.

"What made you put this on this morning? I want to hear about it." William pressed closer to Benji and kissed the underside of his jaw, his stubble waking up Benji's skin.

"It made me feel sexy, I guess. And I, oh shit." William had dropped his hand to pluck at Benji's nipple, nudging a strap out of the way to get to it. Benji tried to keep talking. "I'm a big guy. I work in a traditionally dude-bro-ish industry. It … oh yes … it makes me happy to know I've got this on under my clothes. As if I'm pulling one over on everyone. Gives me an ego boost. Are you sure you like it?"

Benji was so fucking tired of putting parts of himself away for fragile, childish, little men, but he couldn't help but ask.

William was practically vibrating out of his skin. His composure was cracking all over the place.

"*Yes.*"

One simple word, and it might have been the sexiest, most validating word Benji had ever heard.

New rule: if a guy couldn't fuck or be fucked by Benji while he was wearing pink lace, then they didn't deserve his frankly fantastic ass. Or mouth. Or hand.

Chapter Four

William's head was a mess of want and fear. He was scared he was going to fuck this up. The way Benji had asked William if he liked this told William this was a sensitive subject for the beautiful man in front of him. It was hard not to just pull Benji close and take him apart.

William was attracted to the unexpected. He enjoyed being surprised because, honestly, it didn't happen very often, but Benji had been surprising the shit out of him from the moment he'd arrived.

Benji's collarbones were calling to William, so he leaned forward in the chair and slid his lips over the sharply jutting bone. The harness strap at Benji's shoulder brushed William's cheek. It was silky and body warm.

"Were you worried?" William asked.

"'Bout what?" Benji's voice had gone lazy and slurred.

"That I wouldn't be into this." William ran a hand lazily over Benji's chest and the pink straps there.

"Yeah."

"Why? You're beautiful."

Benji dropped his head back on a groan, showing off the sexiest Adam's apple William had ever seen. William licked it.

Benji smelled like candy and ginger beer, and it was such a happy scent, so alive and sweet and dirty that William couldn't hold in a rumbly growl.

"Want you in my mouth," Benji said. "Bet I could make you come so fast."

"Yeah? How fast?"

"Five minutes. Tops."

Seeing Benji on his knees, all trussed up in that strappy getup, had William trembling with need. William would be lucky if he made it thirty seconds.

"What are the stakes?" he asked.

Benji lipped lightly at William's foreskin. "If I win, you spoil me. However you want to spoil me."

The hair on William's neck stood on end. "And if you lose?"

"I won't. You won't let me."

William laughed. He wasn't used to playing these types of games, and it wasn't as if he had a bunch of phone battery to spare, but this was a worthy use of it, he thought. He set a timer on his phone for five minutes. "Do your worst."

Benji grinned and held eye contact as he closed his mouth over William's tip.

A weird dizziness hit William as his body flushed hot. "You are so sweet, aren't you?"

Benji moaned, his mouth going slightly sloppy as he took William deeper. Benji had reacted each time William had said something nice. He was starting to get a handle on the gorgeous man in front of him. Benji enjoyed taking orders, and he loved compliments. It was the easiest thing in the world for William to open his mouth and let praise gush out. He wanted to milk all the sounds out of Benji. All the shivers and sighs and moans.

This ten-second blowjob had already outstripped the sex William was used to, and he loved it. Not that he'd had much sex recently. Too busy. Too stressed to enjoy it. Too picky. Too worried about leading on the person he slept with when he didn't have the energy to commit. Wanting commitment more than almost anything in the entire world. He was a mess, basically, and it hadn't been fair to draw other people into that circle of fucked up. But now he was ready.

And what was he doing?

Screwing around with a younger man whom he'd known for less than three hours, a guy who wasn't interested in anything serious. A fake valentine.

Hell, William hadn't slept with a man in years. But here they were, and he refused to regret it.

How could he ever regret it when Benji looked like a piece of high-dollar erotic art? Perfectly tousled. Cheeks a delicious shade of pink. Straps of expensive pink fabric highlighting his shining, tan skin. Mouth full of cock. God, William wished he could take a picture.

Beyond that though, he was enamored by Benji's teasing voice, his sudden bouts of shyness, and his insane courage. William suspected he could find himself with *feelings* for this man if he wasn't careful.

Benji popped off William's cap, giving a bit of extra attention to the foreskin. "Time's ticking, William. You gonna fuck my face or not?"

"Will you let me come on you?" William couldn't believe those words had escaped him. He hadn't planned on them.

"As long as it's not on my face, sure."

"Deal."

William hooked his thumb in Benji's mouth, held it open, and pushed back inside. His fingers curved over Benji's sharp jaw and caressed it. Benji's eyelashes fluttered, and he placed his hands very deliberately on the arms of the chair, ceding even more control to William. William flexed his hips, pressing slightly deeper into Benji's mouth.

"This okay, sweetheart?"

Benji whimpered, nodded, and jutted his face forward, taking William to the root.

"Oh, fuck me. That's good, Benji. You're so good."

Benji pulled back for a breath, then did it again, deep-throating William so perfectly he could hardly control himself.

"Keep doing that. Want you to make me come while I pet you all over, show you how perfect you are." William scraped a hand through Benji's hair, then trailed his hand over the back of Benji's neck, down to his chest, and back up to his armpit.

William had a thing for armpits. There was probably an evolutionary explanation for that. Pheromones or something? He didn't care about the reason. He just knew he liked it.

As his fingertips skimmed over Benji's sensitive skin, he focused on Benji's reaction. Some people hated it. They were too ticklish there, or it was too weird for them.

Benji let out a gut-wrenching moan—a moan that was satisfyingly muffled by William's cock. It was an orgasm noise. Or an almost-orgasm noise. Which was the fastest way to make William come.

Lingerie. Noises. Armpits. Maybe that was William's knockout punch, because a throbbing pleasure radiated out from the base of his spine to the pit of his stomach. His balls ached.

"Close, baby," William whispered. He fucked into Benji's mouth hard three, then four times.

Benji quaked and tried to take William deeper, his noises dirty and desperate.

William ripped Benji off his cock almost viciously. Benji cried out at the loss, his lips wet and red and puffy, his eyes wide and dazed.

William dropped his palm to his spit-soaked cock and stroked himself twice before painting Benji's chest and neck with his spunk. It fell in pulses over the pink silk straps of Benji's harness, dripping down his pecs onto his abs.

Pleasure rained down on William's body from every

direction, making him feel heavy and sated and whole. Once the last shiver had traveled through him, William cupped Benji's face with both hands. "God, look at you."

A sudden shrill ringing made William jump, but Benji didn't flinch at the sound of the timer.

No, Benji smiled up at him and said, "I won."

<hr>

Winner winner, chicken dinner.

Benji hadn't realized how much he'd love splooge on his chest. It wasn't normally his thing.

William's adoring gaze helped. It was romantic. Romantically fucking dirty.

Benji wanted to crawl into William's lap and kiss him, but William hadn't kissed him on the mouth yet. What if there was a reason for that? Maybe William didn't kiss his random hookups?

Benji wasn't certain he wanted this to be random, not after William had said, "Like *you*. Like you in it," when Benji had first revealed his harness.

This felt personal.

And weren't they fake valentines? If you couldn't kiss your valentine, who could you kiss?

Maybe this really wasn't such a great idea.

As William ran a hand through the come on Benji's chest, pressing it into his skin, Benji was terrified he wouldn't be able to keep up anymore. There was a quiet intensity to William. A subtlety. One Benji wasn't sure he could reach or understand.

Or, maybe it wasn't that Benji *couldn't* keep up. Maybe it was that he was too scared to. There had to be a reason Benji usually fell for immature shitbags, right? Because even a five-minute blowie with someone who was not an immature shitbag was overwhelming. Like a rush of water and good feelings and fear drowning him. Confusing him.

He was in over his head. He realized it so suddenly, so absolutely that it terrified him.

Exhilarated him.

William pulled Benji to his feet and efficiently divested him of his overalls until he was standing there in nothing but a pink lace jock, the body harness that clipped to said jock, and blue wool socks. (It *was* February. Wool socks were a must.)

William stared down at Benji's underwear for an extended beat. The jock was boxer-brief style, and the lace was fairly opaque, so they weren't Benji's most revealing pair of panties. From the front.

"Heavens, you are gorgeous."

"You are too." Benji's words seemed to startle William, because he glanced up, his eyes wide.

"I'm going to spoil you rotten." William licked a stripe up the shallow dip between Benji's pecs, gathering up the jizz there. Then he spun Benji around. "Oh. Hello. I was *not* expecting that."

William gave Benji's exposed cheeks a squeeze. A draft of chilly air rushed over Benji, and he shivered.

"Are you cold, baby?" William asked.

"A bit." God, but Benji was a sucker for endearments.

William unbuttoned his shirt and shed it before

pressing against Benji's back. When their skin slipped together, they both groaned. William kissed Benji's ear. Then the hinge of his jaw. Then the join of his shoulder and neck.

"Kneel down," William whispered in Benji's ear.

"Oh." Benji's breath hitched in his throat, and he followed directions. He loved following directions. It felt like a revelation that William was letting him.

William nudged Benji forward until his knees were on the edge of the hearth. Then he reached over Benji to touch the brick header directly above the fireplace, then the screen in front of it.

"Put your hands right here. It won't burn you," William said. "Yeah, so perfect."

The brick was warm to the touch but not blistering. The heat from the fire bled into him slowly. The rug cushioned his knees, and his hands rested above the firebox, his body an arc over the fireplace. The fire had burned down to embers behind the screen.

This scene would be perfect for his secret stash of lingerie photos, but he didn't have the guts to pause the proceedings and ask William to play photographer.

"Warmer?" William asked, kneeling behind Benji.

"Yes."

"Too hot?"

"No. It's great. Hot but in a sexy way."

Warmth bathed his skin, and he dropped his head between his arms. A drop of sweat rolled down the back of his neck and through the ditch between his shoulder blades.

William must have spotted the droplet because he followed the path with his tongue, a groan on his lips.

"You're so pretty, sweetheart. Your skin is all hot and rosy and glowing from the fire. And fuck, you smell sexy. Spread those beautiful legs for me and arch your back … That's it."

Benji was helpless to do anything but follow orders, his butt sticking out, his palms on the fireplace.

William went to his knees behind Benji, grabbed a fistful of harness and a handful of ass, spread Benji open, and licked over his hole. Sparks burst behind Benji's eyelids. Red sparks. Red, like love and lust and heat. That type of red. Sex red.

Good sex red.

"Oh God, oh God," Benji whispered, his voice thready and thin. He couldn't remember the last time he'd had this. The last time he'd had sex that wasn't stilted, that didn't make him feel calculating and fake. Damn, he'd been having taupe sex.

Normally he'd be worried or insecure or too in his head, but William used his hold on the straps at Benji's spine to pull Benji to his mouth, and Benji couldn't be anything but blown the fuck away.

He'd wanted this for so long. Had wanted to be accepted. To be free.

William made a humming, desperate sound, and sweat exploded over Benji's skin. He needed a hand on his cock, but he loved being serviced. Didn't want it to end, and he'd come too fast if he touched himself. He'd dissolve like cheap candy, then it would be over.

Benji couldn't bear for this to be over yet.

William pushed the tip of his tongue inside him, and it knocked loose Benji's remaining reservations. He cried out and slapped the brick.

"Yeah, honey. Get loud. You like this?" William licked over him roughly. Thoroughly.

"I do … Oh hell."

Benji liked it, and liked it, and *loved* it for long, perfect minutes until he felt so relaxed he could have melted. But also, if anyone *looked* at his dick wrong, he'd pop off. William was making gruff, growly noises again, and his spit was running down the inside of Benji's thighs, soaking the straps of the jock.

William rubbed a thumb over Benji's entrance. "Can I finger you?"

"Uh. Sure. I mean, I love the rimming. You could do that forever."

"Think my mouth would get tired."

"True. What a shame. Yes, finger me."

William laughed and pressed a long, thick finger inside Benji.

It stung a bit because there was nothing but spit for lube, but Benji had always been into that, both the spit and the roughness.

Everything got dizzying after that. William sat up, the heat from his body at Benji's back again. The wet warmth of William's lips on his neck. The piercing, filling thrust of William's fingers. The satisfying stretch that left him wanting bigger and harder. The electric shock of a press against that hot spot inside him. The comfort of a strong arm holding him up.

Benji's own arms went weak, and William gathered him close. And, damn, did Benji love a man who could catch him before he crumbled. And he was fucking crumbling.

William rotated them, laying Benji down on the rug on his back, then crawled between Benji's legs, spit on his own fingers, and pushed them back in.

"I need … Oh no … William, please, I need …"

"What do you need?" William smiled. That easy, charming, unicorns-are-real smile. A smile that let Benji in on a secret.

"A cock," Benji blurted.

William's smile turned fierce and satisfied and possessive. He pressed his groin lightly against the inside of Benji's thigh. "I'm older than you. I'll be out of commission a bit longer."

Benji shook his head, trying to clear it, but it didn't work. "A dildo."

William froze for a second before saying, "I don't really have one handy."

"Everyone should own a dildo, William."

William pressed his laugh into Benji's knee before leaning over him, keeping his fingers firmly planted. They grinned at one another, their lips almost grazing. Benji would take a kiss over a dildo right about then, but it was a close call.

"I bet you've got one upstairs in that duffle, don't you?" William asked.

So, like, ninety percent of Benji wanted the kiss. Ten percent wanted the Swamp Monster Everglides dildo he had in his bag.

"Three. Three dildos." Benji was mesmerized by William's lush mouth. *Kiss me. Kiss me.* A kiss was better than Swampy. He was practically screaming the words in his head.

"I can go get one," William said. His breath tickled Benji's chin.

"No. Don't leave." *Me. Don't leave me*, Benji wanted to say. "Next time."

Kiss me. Kiss me.

Benji's breath was stuttering now. William pulled his fingers out and shoved them back in, lighting up all Benji's nerve endings. Benji was shaking, his back muscles strung taut, his legs trembling.

"Please, William."

"Tell me what you want."

Benji opened his mouth, his gaze snagging on William's lips. He didn't want to have to ask for a kiss. That felt silly somehow, and everything had been perfect up until that moment. He didn't think he could handle a rejection.

William lifted his free hand to Benji's mouth, brushing his thumb over Benji's bottom lip. "Yes?" William asked. "That what you want?"

Benji nodded, desperate for it. "Please."

"Me too."

William pressed his lips to Benji's chin, then the corners of his mouth. Benji threaded his fingers in

William's neat hair, trying to mess it up and hold him where Benji wanted him. The firelight gilded William's cheekbones, and his dark brown eyes glowed behind his lenses. A groan rumbled out of William, and he crashed his mouth down on Benji's. Their teeth clacked together. William's glasses knocked into Benji's face. The angle was awkward, what with William still fucking him gently with his fingers, and it seemed like there were a million hands in the way, but it was also perfect.

William's kiss turned gentle but demanding, and Benji was taken over by it. He was just excitement and taste and sticky, sweet desire.

William pressed closer and his hipbone brushed Benji's cock through its lace prison. Benji writhed, attempting to get more contact. William ripped his mouth away.

"You are a distraction and a half. I want to watch you. Want to watch you until you come apart for me." William licked the sweat off Benji's shoulder, then dipped his head and kissed the stretch of skin below Benji's armpit.

He'd never had a guy target his armpit, but it was the second time William had done so. It sent a ticklish, jumpy sensation to Benji's stomach. He groaned, wanting to be touched there harder. Or maybe lighter. Or wetter. He simply knew it felt weird and good. Benji certainly hadn't expected William to teach him things about his own body, but lifelong learning was a noble pursuit. He'd heard that from a librarian once.

William sat up suddenly and splayed Benji's legs. He thrust his digits inside Benji's ass. With his other hand,

William reached for Benji's cock, gripping him through the delicate lace. Benji's muscles tightened, pleasure pooling in his balls, in his ass. The lace was silky and petal soft against him but textured enough to add intensity.

He gasped, heat flushing his face and washing his vision red. "Make me." The words burst from him, surprising him. He didn't know where they'd come from, but they made his cock throb. "Yes, please. Oh fuck. Force me to … make me, William, please."

"I've got you, baby."

William rubbed him hard over his jock, pushed fingers against his prostate, and Benji's world split in two as he came. Part of him was all pleasure and noise and the release of tension and warm, fuzzy, sexy feelings. And the other was grounded in the earthiness of the moment. The scent of dirty sex. The hot pulse of his heartbeat in his cock and ass. The spit drying around his open, panting mouth. The sticky come seeping through his lacy underwear.

It felt too real. Like too much. Too good considering it had only taken some fingers in his ass and a few strokes over his underwear for him to bust harder than he'd ever, ever busted.

Chapter Five

William got Benji a wet washrag. Semen had bubbled through the delicate pink lattice of Benji's jockstrap, darkening the fabric. It was the sexiest thing William had ever seen.

He wanted to continue to spoil Benji, which, to be honest, was an unusual emotion for him. In the past, after sex, he'd been admittedly interested in getting back to work. Or catching a few hours of precious sleep. With Benji, he kind of wanted to cuddle. Had Valentine's Day infected him, like a germ?

Benji looked at the washrag for a few seconds before taking a hiccupping breath. William's whole world recalibrated.

He kneeled next to Benji, scared to touch him.

"Benji, what's wrong?"

"I don't know." Benji said this with a fair degree of panic and embarrassment in his voice. "I've never done that, but I've wanted it for so long."

William's heart jumped to his throat. He started to reach a hand toward Benji's cheek, but checked himself. "Can I touch you?" He tried to keep his voice even, but on the inside, he was in what-the-fuck mode.

Benji frowned, his eyes bright. "Of course."

William placed his hand on the side of Benji's neck, caressing Benji's jaw with the pad of his thumb. "What haven't you done before? I'm so sorry if I pushed you or—"

"No. I didn't mean—ugh. Sorry." Benji shook his head. "I've never had sex while wearing this shit." He gestured to himself. To the harness and come-soaked underwear.

"Oh." In hindsight, William should have suspected that. "What did you think of it?"

Benji gazed at him, his blue eyes serious and shimmery in the light of the dying fire. "It felt like it's supposed to."

"What do you mean?"

"It felt like I expected it to. Which is reassuring. I hadn't built it up in my head for no reason. It ..." Benji took in another one of those stuttering breaths. William kissed him lightly, chastely, trying to comfort him. When he pulled back, Benji kept his eyes closed. "It was wonderful. I want to do it again."

"Then we'll do it again. We'll do it so many times."

A grin slowly spread over Benji's face, and he opened his eyes. "Did you like it?"

"I think the word *like* would be underselling it."

"Cool."

Benji finally scrubbed the wet cloth over the dried come on his chest before peeling his harness and underwear off to finish cleaning himself up.

William indulged in some light staring. Benji, fully naked, was something else. He was magnificent all wrapped in pretty straps and lace. He was sweet and interesting in his overalls. But naked? Damn. Benji was so unselfconscious. So comfortable. His big athletic body, his wild blond hair, his cock resting against his thigh, the bubble butt that jiggled as he went about the very mundane task of wiping spunk out of his pubic hair.

"What now?" Benji asked suddenly, his voice clipped.

Perhaps not as comfortable as William had thought.

"Whatever you want now," William said, meaning it.

Maybe it was because there was nothing else that could pull at his attention. Not his business partner, Tina. Not the Post-V-Day Bach Auction at Mount—their version of a bachelor auction—that was an absolute thorn in his side. Not the meals he'd missed because he'd been too busy or the phone calls he'd forgotten to return or the bloodbath of his unread emails. Maybe it was because Valentine's Day was right around the corner and loneliness had doused him like a second skin.

Whatever the reason, he was enthralled by Benji Holiday.

"I mean, I don't see why it needs to be a big deal. It was fun." Benji's mouth was a tight line.

"It *was* fun," William said, realizing instantly that he needed to play his cards close to his chest. Maybe the fake valentine thing was an idea Benji had pulled out of nowhere to give them an excuse to have sex. Who knew if it applied now that the orgasms were out of the way?

Benji didn't respond, but he did tug his overalls back on, no shirt, no underwear. So sexy.

William grunted—real smooth—and stalked back into the office. His body felt loose and sated and … cold. Dumb power outage. He put his pajamas back on, decorum be damned. When he returned to the living room, the space was empty and the fire had nearly burnt down to nothing, so he stoked it back to life. Benji appeared a few minutes later. He'd donned a huge neon-orange fleece blanket over the overalls.

"Nice blanket," William said. Smooth, again.

Benji smiled, his eyes teasing. "It's a poncho. Obviously. Nice pajamas. I like you in pajamas. You're not so —" He bit his lip shyly.

"So what?"

"Intimidating, I guess. You're a bit of a frowny guy. The pajamas make you look comfy frowny. Like an angry dog in a cozy sweater." Benji's eyes became brighter the longer he spoke. He was goading William. And God, William wanted to be goaded.

He stalked toward Benji, whose grin widened. William lifted a palm to Benji's cheek, trying to clearly broadcast his intent. Benji's body swayed toward William slightly, and his eyes fluttered closed.

"I'm going to kiss you," William said. He swept his thumb over Benji's cheekbone, over a light, almost invisible, dusting of freckles on his cheek.

"Okay."

"Then we're going to lie on that big-ass couch. I'm going to read and you're going to waste the rest of the charge on your phone. And we might nap, but we're definitely going to kiss again after that. That's what I want."

"Sounds romantic."

William didn't know if Benji was kidding or if the wistful tone was real.

Benji didn't open his eyes, but continued, "Romance is for suckers."

So much for real.

William kissed him, shutting him up. William wasn't usually big into kissing, at least not with strangers. He did it, because sometimes it was easier to kiss than to talk, but he could have listened to Benji talk for ages. No, he kissed Benji because Benji deserved to be showered in kisses. To have them rained on him. Because he was fucking gorgeous and looked ridiculous in his weird poncho, and it was cold, and Benji was so hot. And William just wanted their mouths to be pressed together, and for it to not be about sex but about connection. Even if it was ephemeral. Even if it didn't last. He didn't want this kiss —the wet slide of their lips, the ginger-beer taste of Benji's tongue, the humid puffs of their breaths—to be about anything except how fucking romantic it was to kiss this beautiful man by a crackling fire in a house with no fucking lights on.

Benji gasped and went limp and soppy against him. William held him up. Held Benji's face in his palms, his fingers curling around his jaw, his neck, the silky strands of his hair.

"God," Benji breathed. He touched the back of William's hand—the hand that was holding Benji's neck fast, his thumb resting on the most gorgeous Adam's apple in the country. Which was when William realized that his hold was maybe a little too commanding. He might as well have been collaring him, but Benji said, "God," again, and kissed him softly. Delicately, like William might break. Or maybe like Benji was already breaking.

Benji's fingers gripped William's Cornhuskers sweatshirt as if it were a lifeline. William walked him backwards toward the big sofa, not releasing his mouth for a second, making everything sloppy and clumsy. Benji's knees hit the couch and he tumbled backwards onto it, bringing William down with him.

They kissed for long minutes until Benji pulled back and said, "Instagram."

William lifted his head up, dazed. "Huh?"

"I'll browse Instagram, and you can read your boring book."

"Then we'll kiss again."

"Sure. I guess," Benji said, his wide mouth curving into a puckish smile.

William smiled back and pulled a chunky afghan off the back of the couch over them. The fire sparked and hissed, casting shadows through the room, and William reached behind the couch to slide the curtains open wider, giving him enough light to read by. He pulled a book of poems off the side table.

He was too distracted by Benji to focus on the words.

By his candy mixed with dirty sex scent. By the blond hair tickling his nose. By his heat. It felt so good being pressed together on a couch, toes to chests. Benji tucked his head under William's chin and sighed.

Within five minutes, Benji's phone slipped from his palm, landing on William's stomach, and Benji's body went heavier against him. William's breath caught. Benji had fallen asleep on him, which was strange and nice and slightly alarming.

William carefully put Benji's phone into airplane mode to save the battery and placed it on the side table. Benji didn't stir.

William tried to close his eyes, tried to follow Benji into slumber, but he couldn't. His blood was still pumping pure adrenaline, making his skin feel jumpy and his heart pound. It was as if his body knew that something dramatic had happened, and it couldn't decide if it wanted to lean into it or run.

William's heart wanted to lean. To wallow. To enjoy. But his mind knew better.

Benji was young. Maybe he was impulsive. Maybe he often jumped into bed—or onto a rug by a fireplace— with men he'd just met. Maybe he often agreed to bizarre Valentine's Day agreements with strangers. It probably wasn't a huge deal to him.

It was a huge deal to William. It wasn't that he hadn't had one-night stands before. He had, but not in years. That was the type of thing he'd left behind in his twenties.

He'd kind of left his *life* behind in his twenties, if he

were honest, but he used to be young and impulsive too. It had been nice to revisit it. Even if this went no further than a hot-shit blowjob and some rimming, it had been nice to experience it.

To experience it with Benji.

Yep. He was fine.

William closed his eyes. A log split and sizzled in the fire. The wind howled against the window.

He opened his eyes. Benji snuffled against his chest, and William melted. He should have put *snuffles in their sleep* on his dating criteria.

He wasn't fine. If this was his only taste of Benji, that would not be fine at all.

Benji rubbed his face against the best pillow ever. It smelled good too, this pillow. Like pricy aftershave and jizz.

His head shot up, and he met the dark eyes of William O'Dare. William had taken his glasses off, and his eyes looked sleepy and large and unguarded without the specs.

Not a pillow, then, but William's firm, perfect chest.

"How long have I been holding you cuddle hostage?" Benji whispered.

"Not long."

William rubbed a hand over the back of Benji's neck, sending a wash of tingly heat through him.

Benji's resolve to crawl off this beautiful man

dissolved completely. He slumped back onto William's abdomen. So hard yet so comfortable.

"Like ten minutes?"

"Like an hour and a half."

Benji yelped. "I slept on top of you for an hour and a half!"

"Yes."

"Oh no. I'm such a jerk. Did you sleep too?"

William was silent for a long beat before he shrugged and said, "Yes."

"Liar."

"It was like dozing. Relaxing here with you, not worrying about … well, anything."

"What do you normally worry about?" Benji asked.

"Work."

"Blah. Boring."

William laughed and touched Benji's chin. "It can be, but it's been the only thing in my life for a very long time."

William's serious gaze sent a shot of fear from Benji's heart to his fingertips. This was getting a little heavy, and they needed some ground rules. *Benji* needed ground rules, or he was going to get his hopes up.

He'd get his hopes up or get his heart broken. Either way, he was a total sucker for assholes who were married to their jobs. Or married to other men. He'd fallen into that trap once too.

God, guys sucked sometimes.

"Will. Can I call you Will?"

"Wish you wouldn't," William said with a laugh.

"Fine. William. What are we doing?"

Suddenly, William seemed very interested in the thick curtains behind the couch, his gaze shifting away from Benji. "Cuddling. Or cuddle hostaging?"

"That's not what I meant."

A small, unhappy smile marred William's stern face and he wrinkled his big nose. Benji adored that nose, especially when it wrinkled up like that.

"I know," William said. "I wasn't planning on a fake valentine this weekend."

Benji frowned and took a deep breath. He hadn't been planning on fucking a stranger either. He definitely hadn't been planning on cuddling with one. Or being a fake valentine, but he'd suggested it, and here they were. Ground rules. He needed them!

"I have a problem," Benji blurted. William frowned. Now they were frowning at each other like two very unhappy cuddlers. "It's a personal problem. A love-life problem. And I've been trying to solve it. Trying to figure myself out. To figure out how to be healthy when it comes to relationships and friendships and boundaries. I'm worried I just fucked that up."

William let out a shuddery sigh. A disappointed sigh, maybe? Or a scared one? Then William lifted a hand and cupped Benji's cheek. "Sweetheart. Can I call you sweetheart?"

"Wish you would. Like, all the time," Benji admitted.

"Sweetheart, whatever you're worried about, I'll help if I can. If you're freaked out about what we did, we can fix it. I'm not here to hurt you or complicate things for you. It'll be okay. If I can make it okay, I will."

"Gah, you're too much."

William snorted a laugh. "What's the problem? You said you have a problem. Tell me what it is, and we'll go from there."

Benji nodded and closed his eyes, trying to shape the words in his head, his heart, into something that made sense. Into a sentence that wasn't pathetic, emotional word vomit.

"I … I have a tendency to get involved with guys who aren't very good for me. I'm a people pleaser, see."

"Okay. Go on." William slipped his fingers into Benji's hair and massaged gently.

Benji kept his eyes closed. It was easier that way. To pretend as if he were speaking to his therapist. Or his sister. Or a wall. Not this nice-as-hell hottie.

"My parents weren't around. I think that's where my people-pleasing comes from." Oh God, he was really spilling the beans. "That's my theory, at least. I'm desperate to please the people in my life so they won't up and fucking bail. If I can contort myself into exactly the right shape, whatever asshole I've attached myself to won't leave me." Oversharing alert. He took a big, gasping breath, on a roll now. "If I stop wearing my favorite clothes. If I put away my lingerie. If I pretend to like IPAs. If I delete my Instagram. If I pretend that I don't mind being cheated on. If I—"

"Hey, whoa. It's okay." William gently cradled Benji's

face with both hands, and Benji realized he was trembling. "Deep breath."

Benji nodded and kept talking. "I'm an easy mark, I think. For controlling dickheads." He *hoped hoped hoped* William didn't end up being a controlling dickhead. "I must have a bullseye on my forehead that says 'pushover.'"

"I'm so sorry if I was too controlling."

"No! Oh God, that's not what I meant. That's one of the problems. I enjoy giving up control in bed but not outside it. It's outside of bed where it hurts, you know?"

"Yeah, I do."

"I've been on a dating moratorium lately, besides some unwise booty calls with my ex. Loneliness is a hell of a drug. Makes me do all kinds of stupid shit."

William kissed Benji's forehead. William was a great listener, which meant Benji kept talking and talking and talking.

"I liked what we did earlier," Benji said. That felt like a big admission.

"I did too."

"I think I want to keep doing it." That felt like an even bigger admission.

Silence stretched between them for long, embarrassing seconds. Benji had fucked this up. He was sure of it. But William was still touching him, and Benji wanted to be called "sweetheart" at least one more time.

Finally, William said, "I think this could benefit us both."

"How?"

"It's fun, for one. I haven't had any fun in a very long time. We can focus on the fun and leave the heavy stuff at the door. No room for heavy when there's no electricity. That's a rule I just made up."

"I like that rule." Benji pressed his forehead to William's throat.

"And I've been trying to jump back into the dating game, but I've lost my mojo."

"No!" Benji said, shocked. "You have all the mojo."

William gave him a smacking kiss on the cheek. "I think this fake valentines thing could help me be with someone without the pressure. Get me back in the game, so to speak. It will get us both back in the game. You can be with someone who absolutely *does not* want you to change an iota. You're beautiful and funny and you deserve to be appreciated. You can be wholly yourself. No masks. Just you. We can practice."

"Sex practice?"

"Dating practice. But also, yes, let's have lots of sex."

It would feel good to simply be himself and to be completely honest. To not be lonely on Valentine's Day.

"Fake valentines," Benji whispered. "We can be totally loving and attentive to each other through this weekend. Really put our hearts into it."

"For the weekend."

"Yeah. I would be the best weekend valentine."

"What about after?"

They stared at each other, and Benji wondered how clearly William could actually see him without his glasses.

"I feel like there's a very wrong answer to that question, but I don't know what it is," Benji admitted.

William's expression softened. "That's okay."

"Let's agree that … there are no expectations beyond the weekend."

"Okay. I can live with that."

Benji took a big ol' breath. "But it's not off the table."

Chapter Six

B enji couldn't help but worry that he was wasting precious time. They only had the weekend. But lounging in a cold room with William's strong arms wrapped around him was now one of his top three ways to spend an evening, so he couldn't complain too much. The number one and two top ways to spend an evening would probably involve sex. Or food. One—blowjobs. Two—pizza. Three—cuddling. Maybe he could finagle William into a top-five situation.

Four—watching Netflix shows about Australian AirBnBs.

Five—mutual masturbation? Hmmm, he'd have to think on it. Examine the data points.

"What are we going to eat tonight?" Benji whispered.

"I have bread and peanut butter."

"Boring. Is DoorDash a thing out here in the sticks?"

William kissed the top of Benji's head. Benji shivered

in pleasure. He loved how affectionate William was being with him. He'd never had that.

He'd have to remember to ask for it in the future. With whomever he was with.

"There's a local pizza place. I think everything in town has power. It only affected the properties in the lake quadrant."

"There's a town?"

"Sort of. There's an antique store, a gas station, a school, and a pizza place. The pizza place is in the gas station."

Benji hummed. Gas station pizza was perhaps not worthy of the number-two spot on his best ways to spend an evening list, but it was still in the top ten. He wasn't picky when it came to heaven's pie.

"Do they deliver?"

"Yes. And I have a coupon. Someone left a flyer on the door."

"Nothing better than discounted gas station pizza. Let's do it!" Benji crawled off the sofa ungracefully—William let out an *oomph* as Benji's knee narrowly missed his stomach. Then Benji tossed William his phone. "You call. My phone's about dead. I'll eat any pizza as long as it doesn't have *fruit* on it. Otherwise, surprise me."

William smiled his indulgent smile and walked into the kitchen to make the order. Benji heard him say, "Yes, I'd like the Sweet Treat Two-Topping Pizza for Two. I have a coupon."

Benji decided to explore some of the nooks and crannies of the living room while William was occupied. Now that he'd had William's dick in his mouth, he wanted to know more about the man.

Benji made a circuit of the dim room. It was kind of boring. The bookcase was full of nonfiction and poetry. The walls were gray. The mantel was bare. The afghan on the couch was a muted mauve that clashed with the brown couch. The rug was from Target. Benji could recognize a good Target purchase from a mile away.

Benji skirted the kitchen counter so he could see William in the back corner of the kitchen. He was giving his information to the pizza place.

There was a door off the small breakfast nook. Benji pushed it open gently. He could feel William's eyes on him, but William wasn't stopping him.

It was a dark office, but a well-used one. It felt lived-in in a way the rest of the house didn't. The desk was littered with files and papers and two big computer monitors. There was a black futon that was in the sofa position, but it had clearly been slept on, what with the pillow and messy tumble of blankets covering it.

William's suitcases were in this room too, open to display neatly folded clothes. A weird sort of protective anger flowed through Benji.

He wheeled around and marched back into the kitchen. William was no longer on the phone, but he was standing still as a statue.

"You use that office as a bedroom, don't you?"

William nodded.

"But … but William! The room that you gave me—that should be your room. It's beautiful. It's obviously the master suite. That room"—he gestured toward the office —"doesn't even have a fucking closet. You're staying on the futon, but I'd bet my lingerie savings that you don't fold it out when you sleep."

"I don't."

Benji stalked toward William. "Why do you sleep in there?"

"It's easier. When I'm here, I usually work late, and it's convenient to just … lie down in there. Pizza will be here soon."

"Don't change the subject by talking about pizza, you trickster. Surely you don't sleep in your office at home. Why would you do it at your vacation home?"

William's expression went suspiciously blank. Benji was getting familiar with that look. He suspected it was William's boardroom look. If William had to do stuff in boardrooms. Benji had no idea what William's job entailed, but that wasn't the point.

"Oh. My. God! You do sleep in your office at home."

The corners of William's mouth twitched up. "I would never."

Benji lunged toward him, wrapping his arms around William's shoulders. "You do, you do, you do! You are a workaholic. A bad one. You need treatment."

William's hands landed on Benji's hips beneath the poncho, holding him like he was delicate. "I'm fine. The office in my apartment is actually the spare bedroom. So … there."

"Does this spare bedroom actually have a bed?"

William hesitated. "It has a chaise lounge, but it's as

comfortable as my bed. And I only sleep in there every so often. Twice a week, maybe."

"I guess that's better than sleeping at an office that's not located in your own home."

A red flush crawled up William's neck.

"Oh. My. God!" Benji said again.

"I know, but—I know." William dropped his head onto Benji's chest and nuzzled in.

"Don't distract me by being cute."

"You're the cute one."

Bubbly, happy warmth spread through Benji's chest. "Don't distract me with compliments."

William huffed and tipped his head back, giving Benji a stern glare. "You will always get compliments from me. You'll have to learn not to be distracted by them, sweetheart."

"You're a workaholic. Check yes or no."

William rolled his eyes. "Yes."

"Is that why you need practice dating?"

"Yes."

"Your boyfriends are the mistress to your job. Second fiddle. Your dirty secret." Benji swooned dramatically.

"Oh, goodness gracious, that's enough," William said, but he was laughing. "And not exactly true."

"How isn't it true?"

"I'm not gay. My last partner wasn't a *boy*friend."

"Oh." Benji could kick himself for assuming.

"That a problem?"

"Of course not. Want to talk about it? And don't

think that our little foray into Sexuality 101 is going to get you out of talking about your job."

William pulled Benji closer, their bodies flush. "I'm not big into descriptors."

"Okay."

"Okay?"

Benji nodded, not wanting to push. "Yeah. I know lots of people who don't do labels."

William smiled. "I don't offer up labels very often, but pansexual feels the closest. It's complicated, and I don't like having to explain."

"I like complicated, and I *hate* explainers."

William snorted, which was the most endearing type of laugh. Benji's new goal was to get William to snort all the time.

"Anyway, the pizza should be here in—"

"Nope. Not so fast. I'm gay. Now that our rainbow stripes are out in the open, let's talk about your job."

William groaned. That was as nice of a noise as the snorting. Benji definitely wanted to hear him groan again, but in a much different context.

"I poured my fears and issues out on you earlier. Fair is fair," Benji said, even though he was thinking about sinking to his knees.

"Fine." William considered him for a long moment. "I'm lonely. I've been married to my job for so long that I have no idea how to be a good partner, but I want to be. I want to find someone who is right for me, and whom I'm right for too. I've hurt a lot of people in the last ten years. My career came first. It came before my family, before my friends, before anyone I dated. And I don't regret that, exactly. I love my job. But I'm at a place where I can slow down, and I don't want to do that alone."

Benji didn't think practicing the valentine gig this weekend was that great of a test for William. The power was out. It was impossible for William to work without electricity. The real test would be if he could be an attentive valentine when his job was tempting him away.

But Benji sure as hell wasn't going to say *that*. He'd rather live in their weird little paradise.

"See, that wasn't so hard, was it?"

"You have no idea," William said, his eyes almost sad and pleading, and Benji melted.

Benji leaned down to kiss William. He was taller, but William took control of the kiss immediately, gripping Benji's chin firmly.

Benji's legs were jelly, so he let gravity pull him down. Science was great. He hit his knees.

William groaned again.

Benji grinned. He was in total lust with that groan.

"Have you had enough time to recover, old man?"

"It's been hours, smart-ass."

"Oh yeah. Keep talking dirty to me." Benji yanked William's flannel pants to his knees.

The doorbell rang.

"Noooo," Benji whined. He thunked his head onto William's thigh.

William threaded his hand into Benji's hair and tilted his head back. Benji's body lit up like a pinball machine.

"Dinner first, you beautiful sl—" William bit the word off before it escaped.

"Say it. I'll like it," Benji whispered.

William watched him closely. "You beautiful slut."

Benji loved it. He nodded and panted and generally forced himself not to deepthroat the man in front of him.

William grinned and went to get the pizza.

Chapter Seven

Talking to Benji was fun because *Benji* was fun, but William had not enjoyed the job conversation. Benji discovering that William slept in his office poked at every insecurity and point of weakness William had. Every mistake he'd made in the past.

Thank God for the distraction of pizza.

He swung the front door open only to be assaulted by roses, a big balloon, and the strong scent of burnt cheese.

"What the—" Had he accidentally ordered a Valentine's Day special?

"I have a Sweet Treat Two-Topping Pizza for Two for William?" the gangly delivery boy said.

He took the pizza box from the teenager. The small bouquet of roses was lying caddy-corner across the greasy box. Then the teenager handed him a wine bottle. No, not a wine bottle. A sparkling-cider bottle. There was a huge mylar, heart-shaped balloon tied to the neck with the words "I Adough You" scrolled across it in blue marker. Lastly, the delivery boy passed over a large brownie wrapped in cellophane.

"This is … very nice. Thank you. Here's the coupon," William said.

Benji squeezed in behind him in the entryway. "Wow, babe. You shouldn't have. This is so romantic." He took the cider from William and cradled the bottle, the balloon banging off the top of the doorframe.

The teenager's eyes went wide, and he grinned like he'd been handed the keys to a Maserati. "Hi! Cool. You're boyfriends?"

Benji jumped in. "We're valentines. That's why we've planned such an amorous meal. Meat Lovers pizza and gas station brownies and apple juice. Yum."

"Oh no. It's not Meat Lovers," the delivery boy said, flustered suddenly. He pulled the receipt out of his pocket. "It's only Italian sausage and green peppers. Is it supposed to be a Meat Lovers? Oh shit. I mean, *shoot*. That's the third time I've delivered the wrong pizza *today*!"

"No. I'm sorry. This is right," Benji said, stricken and remorseful, which was deserved, what with sending their teenage delivery boy into such a panic. "This is what we ordered. I was just being …"

"Not funny," William finished for him.

Benji buried his laugh in William's shoulder.

"Wow. Okay. That's cool. Please don't tell my boss I cussed." The teenager was staring at them avidly.

"We won't. I promise." William pulled cash out of his wallet and thrust it at the teen. "Thanks."

"Wow," the boy said again as the door closed. William hadn't counted out the bills. He'd probably overpaid.

"Who needs fancy dinners when they have Pecker's Pizza Town?" Benji asked.

William couldn't hold in his snort. "It's Peter's Pizza Town. Come on. Let's eat."

The house was darkening as the sun sank lower in the sky, but the fireplace gave off enough light to see each other while sitting cross-legged on the rug with the pizza box between them.

"That kid acted like he'd never seen a queer couple before," Benji said, after they'd both downed three slices apiece.

"Yeah, well. This is a small town."

"Rural queers exist. I read an article about them once." Benji's lips curled into a teasing smile.

"I know. I grew up in a small town, but—"

"*You did?*"

William had no idea why that was a surprise. "Yes."

"Is that why you bought this lake house in the boonies? You missed the middle-of-nowhere feel? Because I have to tell you, there are much snazzier lakes around. This one is basically a big pond."

"I think that's the definition of a lake, isn't it?"

Benji pointed a piece of crust at him. "Don't distract me with knowledge. That's as hot as the compliments."

"I bought this house because I thought it'd be smart for me to have an escape from the hamster wheel of my job."

"Oh yeah? How's that working out for you there, hotrod?"

"Not great," William admitted. "Until the power went out."

"So sad. Now you have to spend the night paying attention to me."

"Spoiling you. I think I'm coming out ahead in this scenario. The Bach Auction at Mount might not have all the slots filled next weekend, but it was worth it to watch you take off those overalls."

"Wait. Do you own Mount?"

"Yeah. It's our newest."

"Holy crap. I like that bar. It has retro arcade games."

"That's good. You're essentially an exact match to the customer profile I created two years ago."

"I'm over the club scene, but that one is nice." Benji took a big gulp of sparkling cider, straight from the bottle. It still had the balloon tied to it. He had to hold the string in one hand so it didn't get in his way.

He passed the bottle over. William took a slug.

It was too sugary for him. He'd rather taste it on Benji's lips anyway. William put the bottle down and leaned over the pizza box, praying Benji wouldn't leave him hanging.

They were fake valentines, after all.

Benji didn't. Benji met him halfway. His mouth tasted of spicy meat and bubbly apple juice, and it was wonderful. William cupped Benji's cheek.

"You always smell like candy," William whispered, like it was a secret, right onto Benji's lips.

"My body wash is called Watermelon Fantasy."

William almost asked Benji why in the world he'd chosen a watermelon-scented body wash but found he didn't really care. It was perfect on him.

Benji brushed the pizza box out of the way and crawled into William's lap. William caught him, spreading the orange poncho out around their legs.

"We're great at this romantic bullshit," Benji said, his breath whispering over William's neck, making him shiver.

"I think we're just great at making out. No complaints though."

Benji leaned back and frowned. "I'm romantic as hell."

"I wasn't accusing you of not being. It was more a commentary on our meal of choice."

"This has been an awesome meal."

"I hadn't had pizza in ages."

"I bet you haven't had fun in ages. Oh! Do you eat the same thing every day?"

"Not for dinner."

That comment made Benji grin for some reason. He smacked a kiss on William's mouth, loud and obnoxious and amazing.

"What do you eat for *lunch* every day?"

William sighed. "A turkey and avocado wrap from the deli across the street from my office. Also carrot sticks."

"Tomorrow, we're eating candy for lunch."

"Oh my God, we are not."

"Valentine's Day candy. It's like regular candy, but in pink wrappers and sold at a markup. Super-special stuff."

Happiness washed through William. He couldn't remember ever feeling so … so exhilarated over a relationship. Even if this was sort of a possibly fake, weekend-only relationship.

William kissed Benji because he was at major risk of saying something bizarre and too revealing.

Please date me for real, Benji.

I like you *like you.*

Stay with me. Give me sunshine and excitement and unexpected laughter and you.

Give me you.

Much better to coax Benji's tongue into his mouth. Better to stifle the crazy impulses sneaking up on him.

"Wanna fuck in a bed this time. Your bed," Benji said.

"The futon?"

"Of course I don't mean the futon!"

"Oh, your bed. Upstairs."

"Yeah, plus we already lit the wood-burning stove up there. It should be warm."

"That was smart of us," William said.

"Very. I'll bring the roses. You figure out the lighting situation."

Benji jumped out of William's lap, easy-peasy like a breakdancer, and jogged up the stairs. Shit, William felt old. He had to go to his hands and knees and stand up slowly. Fucking in a bed was a brilliant idea.

It was dark in the house now that the sun was down. The fire in the fireplace had burnt down to embers, and he'd turned off the kerosene lamp. He closed the screen on the fireplace and made sure it was safe to leave it.

Luckily, William was an overly prepared control freak, so he'd gathered all his candles and put them in a box earlier. They were in the laundry room off the kitchen. He grabbed the box and started up the stairs, moving slowly in the dark. When he finally reached the top floor, he found Benji deconstructing the roses and littering the sheets with petals. He was using precious phone battery to light his way.

"Romance," Benji said, evidently in explanation.

Those poor roses. "We're good at it. I have candles."

"Guess what I don't have," Benji said, taking the box from him.

"What?"

"Condoms. I don't know if we'd need them, but—"

"Oh. There are some in your bathroom. I'll grab them." Further proof that this was meant to be the master suite. William had stocked it with essentials years ago.

"Fabulous." Benji pushed him toward the bathroom. "Stay in there until I'm ready. I'll yell for you."

"Okay." William went. It was midnight dark in the bathroom. He dug around in the drawers under the sink until he found the box of condoms and a bottle of lube.

When William thought of romantic sex, it unrealistically didn't include prep time. The candles were just magically there. The roses didn't have to be torn up for their petals. There weren't all these roadblocks. But that wasn't real, was it? And real sex, with its laughter and stopgaps and delays, was better than a sanitized, idealized version of it.

He wanted to have earthy, funny, messy sex with Benji, and it had been ages since he'd allowed himself to feel that way.

"Okay. Ready," Benji called.

William stepped out of the bathroom and gasped.

Benji had set candles around the room, some on the bedside tables, some sitting in front of the wood-burning stove, some on the ground next to the sliding glass door. It was beautiful.

But not nearly as beautiful as the man sitting on the end of the bed. Benji's legs were covered in black filmy stockings, and he was wearing a long silky navy T-shirt with a loose open neck. A nightie, William's brain provided out of nowhere. The getup wasn't that revealing, but William about swallowed his tongue regardless. He couldn't wait to feel the cool silk under his fingertips. To lift the shirt slowly up Benji's body, unveiling him bit by bit.

In the dancing candlelight, the silk looked like moving water and Benji's legs looked a mile long and the sex toys scattered next to him looked like …

Holy shit, sex toys. So many sex toys.

William didn't have a ton of sex-toy experience. He and Wren had used vibrators when they were together because Wren couldn't get off without vibration. And back in college, when William first realized he might enjoy getting fucked, he'd gone to a porn shop and purchased a dildo. He'd worn the thing out.

But this—holy shit, sex toys. This was another level. One of the dildos was big, green, iridescent … and scaly? And there was a masturbation sleeve and a … well, he had no idea what that thing with the balls was. His ears burned, and the back of his neck prickled with embarrassment. Or maybe excitement. A weird mix of both?

William had no idea what to say, so he did what came naturally in that moment. He fell to his knees in front of Benji and nudged his legs apart with his face. The velvetiness of the stockings against William's cheeks sent a full-body tremble through him.

Benji sucked in a breath and leaned back on his hands, his legs splayed. William ran his nose up Benji's calf to the inside of his thigh. The watermelon scent was both stronger and different here. Slightly musky but still so fucking sweet.

"Tell me about these stocking things," William said.

"What about them?"

"Why do you like them? Why'd you put them on tonight? Whatever you want to tell me while I suck on your nuts."

"Oh God. Okay."

William nosed farther up to the dark shadow between Benji's legs. Benji wasn't wearing underwear. William shifted the silky T-shirt out of his way, the fabric slick to the touch. His palms skimmed over smooth garter straps that were clipped to the stockings. They disappeared under the shirt like a secret treasure. He couldn't wait to discover what they were attached to. Later. He'd reveal it later. He'd unwrap Benji like a fucking gift.

He rolled Benji's balls in his palm, and Benji sucked in a stuttering breath.

"Talk," William said. Benji's head dropped back on a moan.

Benji gulped as William lifted his balls and lapped at the seam behind them. He had no idea how he was expected to talk with William's mouth anywhere near his junk, but he was willing to try.

"The stockings," William said. "I want to hear about them."

"O-oh-kay," Benji said as William laved over the head of his cock. "I love the way the stockings complement the, umm, well, it's a surprise. For you."

William sat up and grinned. "Why did you bring this stuff? I mean, *this* wasn't planned. Between us. So why did you bring it?"

"The pretty underthings are more about self-expression than sex for me. I like the way they make me feel."

William evidently loved that answer because he swallowed Benji down on a throaty groan. After a few seconds, he slurped back up to the tip.

"And the toys?" William asked.

"I planned to spend all my time jerking off in a stranger's house, which, oh fuck. Which is kind of rude, I guess, but I like being rude."

William continued to blow him. Benji let his hands stray to William's thick, wavy hair. He rubbed a thumb through the streak of silver on the high arch of his forehead. Benji was obsessed with that streak.

He must have been quiet for too long—not counting his moans, which were loud and shameless—because William squeezed the ticklish pressure point above Benji's knees.

"Keep going," William said, letting Benji slip from his lips. "I want to know everything." William was tense, a fine and constant tremble moving through his wide shoulders.

He was getting off on Benji's words, but Benji wasn't exactly eloquent when getting his dick sucked. Or ever.

"Okay. Mmmm. Crap. So, like I said, the lingerie isn't sexual for me. Or, maybe, it's only something I associate with sex when I'm in the mood for sex. But I've never worn it while having sex, as you may have realized after I almost cried all over you this afternoon … after you, God … after you made me splooge in my knickers."

William let out a huffing noise, which Benji was certain was a laugh.

"I've always collected lingerie." And taken pictures of himself in it, but William didn't need to know that. "But I only recently started wearing it regularly."

Once he'd decided he didn't need to be what everyone else wanted him to be, he'd started donning it more freely. More often.

"I wear it nearly all the time now," he explained. "For myself. I'm sure there are articles out there about why men enjoy wearing lacy underthings, but I haven't delved that deeply into it." Benji had to slam his eyes shut because William had started touching himself, and seeing his arm move was too much for Benji to handle. "I, yes. Oh God. Okay. I like to feel pretty. It gives me confidence. These stockings make my legs look long and smoothed out, but they also highlight my calf muscles. I'm tall and stacked, and I love how lingerie emphasizes that. That's it!"

It was getting harder to talk, but it was like Benji had just discovered important and integral information about himself, and he couldn't stop the words from pushing at his chest. He gasped them out. "I love … that I feel hot and strong and free when I'm wearing stuff like this. Even in … oh fuck, I'm getting close."

William pulled off with a hard suck and pressed his forehead to Benji's thigh. He seemed overwhelmed, and Benji wanted to soothe him. But he also loved the uncontrolled edge to William's movements, as if he was barely hanging on.

Benji widened his legs, and William leaned in, licking one of Benji's balls into his mouth. The soft, wet warmth made his legs clench and his toes curl in the stockings.

"Can't keep talking, William. It's too good."

William dropped the ball from his mouth, and the sensation echoed up through Benji's groin, filling it with heat. He felt like he could combust.

"That's okay, baby. Sit back and let me spoil you. Try not to come."

"Fuck. Okay."

William alternated between Benji's dick and his sac, changing focus every time Benji got worked up.

It was probably the most frustrating blowjob of Benji's life.

Or the best.

Yes, definitely the best.

William moved his hands past Benji's hip and up to his waist. Benji had been waiting for that. He'd been planning on it.

Almost there. Almost to the—

A loud *thunk* came from the direction of the backyard. William jerked, and thank Cupid, did not bite Benji's dick.

They stared at each other for a long second.

Another *thunk*.

Then an almighty crash.

Chapter Eight

Was William's house cock-blocking them? Benji was suspicious.

"Is your house haunted?" he asked.

William took a deep breath. "I'll go check it out."

Benji didn't really want William to leave, but that was what you did when your house made freaky noises, right? You didn't ignore them.

"Do you have a weapon? Pepper spray maybe?" Benji asked next.

William blinked a few times. "I'll be fine. Behave while I'm gone."

Benji groaned and flopped back on the bed, sex toys and rose petals spilling around him.

Was it poor form to fuck yourself with a dildo when your fake valentine stepped out to deal with ghosts? Or burglars?

Maybe snakes?

William had told him to behave, but he hadn't said *how* to behave.

Badly. That was Benji's vote. He'd behave badly. Then when William got back, he'd make Benji pay for it. He'd withhold Benji's orgasm. Or force him to have one. Or continue to give him the slowest, best blowjob in the universe.

Benji had just started to jerk off when William reappeared. He stood there in the doorway, his jaw slack and his eyes blazing.

"Hi," Benji said.

"Hi. Raccoons."

"Huh?" He pulled his hand off his dick. "Everything okay?"

William prowled toward him, stopping at the edge of the bed. Prowling was such a predatory word. It made Benji think of being hunted. Being bitten.

Being devoured.

It perfectly described William. The way he moved. The harsh lines of his face. The blade of his strong nose. The hungry glint in his eyes.

Prey. Benji wanted to be his prey, all trussed up in something pretty.

"Raccoons knocked over my trashcan. Then the recycling."

"Naughty buggers."

"God, I'd love to take a picture of you. Exactly. Like. That."

Benji must have looked candle-kissed and hot and bothered. "You can."

"What? For real?"

Benji keyed open his phone, checked the battery—ten percent—and handed it over. An odd suffusion of power tripped through his veins. He didn't normally like to be in control, but he felt in control now. He held William in his thrall. He loved it.

William's body was shaking as he kneeled on the edge of the bed. His eyes were bright behind his glasses, candlelight reflecting in them, but his hands were steady on the phone. Benji crossed his knee over his body to cover his dick, but also to show off his ass and the garters on his legs. William tapped on the phone.

"It's dark, but not too dark. Artsy," William said gruffly, examining the screen.

Benji's breath quickened, and the blood in his temples and fingertips began to throb. These photos would be amazing on his secret Instagram, if he ever had the guts to start his secret Instagram account. Or, he could keep these pictures private. Pore over them long after this weekend was done and William had moved on.

William tugged the silky T-shirt higher up Benji's body, finally (fucking finally) revealing the high-waist lacy garter belt. The bottom of the belt hit Benji directly below the belly button, and the black lace popped against his skin. He'd bought this piece when he was twenty-one. It was his first, and he'd rarely worn it. It was special to him, and he didn't want to look too closely at why he'd decided to share it with William.

"Oh. Honey, you're …" William shook his head. "I

can't think of words. Amazing. Gorgeous. Perfect. Fucking perfect. None of them are big enough."

"Syllables are hard," Benji said, trying to pull humor over himself like a shield.

"You're indescribably beautiful, Benji. I am so happy that you accidentally showed up early for the party. No matter what happens after this weekend, thank you. Thank you for being here. For letting me be here with you."

Benji's heart *thunk*ed over like a barrel of recycling. Shit. Why had he decided this was a good idea again? This wasn't practicing dating with a harmless older man. It was sex. And sex in a way that opened up Benji's vulnerabilities and insecurities and old hurts. He'd never had sex like this before.

He scrubbed a forearm over his face.

William grabbed Benji's hand and brought it up to his lips, placing a kiss in the center of his palm. "It's okay."

Benji laughed and said, "*Shit.*" This time out loud. "I feel really exposed and really sexy, and it's kind of scary, but I also like it. And you are so fucking nice. It's not fair. I don't know how to defend myself against it."

"Then don't." William slipped the shirt higher up Benji's torso. He took one last picture, then turned the phone off and placed it on a table beside the bed. "Let me spoil you."

Once, when Benji was a child, his dad had shown up after months of absence. It had been March, but he'd brought them presents, saying they were for Valentine's Day. A band T-shirt and Hot Topic jewelry for Sasha.

Stationary and a sleek Trapper Keeper for Rosie. He'd given Benji a baseball glove. Which had been awesome.

Except the glove had been lefthanded. Benji would have done anything to shape himself into the kid who could have used that glove, but he couldn't make himself lefthanded.

His grandma—their actual guardian—had been livid at his dad for not knowing Benji was righthanded. Benji's dad had gotten defensive and angry and disappeared for another year, leaving Benji feeling responsible for his absence. But Benji had also realized something important that day.

It was better to keep your expectations low, especially with someone who had the power to hurt you.

The memory flashed through Benji's brain. Maybe it had come to him because it was one of the many holiday memories in which one or both of his parents had failed, and being here, all surrounded by Valentine's Day, had knocked it loose. Or maybe it was because this excitement in his stomach felt a little bit like opening that paper bag to see a baseball glove inside. Like Benji was getting his hopes up, was allowing William to get close enough to hurt him.

This whole thing was romantic. The room. The rose petals. The lingerie. The understanding between them.

If William pulled the rug out from underneath him. If William offered him something wonderful, only to backpedal or end up being an asshole ... Well, if that happened, then Benji was wasting this garter belt on an asshole, and that would be a huge shame.

"We can stop," William said softly. "If this is too much. We can go eat the gas station brownie and play Canasta."

"Canasta has too many rules," Benji said staunchly. "I don't want to stop."

Benji had quit betting on his parents. He'd learned his lesson soon after the baseball-glove incident. And he'd quit betting on his ex, and guys like his ex, because he didn't want to have to change himself to be loved.

But if having two wonderfully badass sisters had taught him anything, it was that sometimes people surprised you. Sometimes they were legitimately good.

Benji wanted William to be legitimately good so badly his body ached with it. Even if it only lasted a weekend. Even if it only lasted a night. He was willing to bet on it. To take the chance.

"I don't want to stop," he said again. "Not at all."

William leaned in to place a kiss directly above the lace of the garter belt, like a benediction, and Benji didn't feel so silly for his momentary storm of emotions. William glanced up at him, his eyes wide behind the lenses of his glasses.

"Turn over for me?" he asked.

Benji loved when William was bossy, but the earnest suggestion was just as sweet. He rolled onto his stomach. The crisp cotton sheets against his erection were too delicious to bear, and he couldn't help but press his hips firmly into the bed. He was back in the ballgame now.

One of William's hands landed on Benji's thigh, slipping under the garter and forcing him to spread his legs a bit. William hummed.

Then something tickled the bottom edge of his butt cheek. It moved gently along the join of his leg and buttocks. It wasn't a finger—too flimsy. Wasn't a toy.

Whatever William was holding, he drifted it lightly up Benji's crack to the base of his spine, then back down again. It felt nice, like a tease.

Benji cranked his head around to see. William was fluttering a rose petal over Benji's skin.

There was also a rose petal crushed under his hipbone, feather-soft and silky. And another one under his cheek, filling his nose with its floral, earthy scent.

Benji had never been into roses. They seemed clichéd. Plus, you could get them practically anywhere nowadays. These gas station roses were case in point.

But damn, every time William swept that petal up and down the outside of his crease, Benji's hair stood on end. His heart tripped over and a pleasurable ache spread from the small of his back. Benji was a roses convert. It was probably the single most erotic moment of his life.

Thank God.

Thank God, he'd taken this chance.

Too bad it was spoiled by a door banging open downstairs and a voice calling out, "Willie! We're here to rescue you from your boring life!"

Chapter Nine

"Son of a cock-blocking cupid," William said under his breath.

"Who the fuck is that?" Benji twisted into a sitting position and pulled his silk nightie over his knees. William could have mourned. "And *Willie*?! Can I call you that?"

"No."

This was the absolute worst thing that could have happened. Benji had been emotional. Something big had been going on here. William didn't quite understand what that big thing was, but interrupting it was the *absolute worst thing that could have happened.*

"William?" Wren called again from the front door.

He needed to get down there before she came looking.

"William," Benji said, his voice a panicky echo of hers.

"That's my best friend, Wren. Sounds like she has someone with her."

"Wait. Wren Rebello?" Benji asked.

"Yes."

"Wren Rebello, the lingerie designer, is your best friend. Oh fuck. Duh. That's how you know my sister. Wren designs underwear for Sasha's company."

"Yeah."

"Well, when you go down there, thank her for making this garter belt in my size."

"She designed this?" William placed his hand on Benji's side, touching the belt through his nightie.

Benji nodded. The skin around his eyes was pinched and drawn. "Does them being here change things?"

William almost asked why it would, but he stopped himself. He didn't want to have to explain their fake valentines situation to Wren, but he would. He'd rather explain than make Benji think he was a secret.

"Fuck, of course it does," Benji jumped in before William could respond. "Wren will tell my sister about us, and I don't think I can deal with the questions right now." Benji ran his hands through his hair, dropping his head down to stare at the bed. When he lifted it, his gaze was closed-off and guarded. "Secret fake valentines, then?"

William had been worried about Benji feeling like a secret but hadn't considered what he'd feel like if *he* were the secret. Wasn't great, to be honest.

Footsteps echoed on the stairs. Then a door opening and closing on the second floor.

"Sure." William stood, giving Benji a flyby kiss. "Wait here. I'll be back, and we will finish this. Unless the house is on fire, no other interruption could pull me away."

Benji laughed and fell back into bed like an angel crashed to earth. "Don't jinx the house. I'm convinced it has a sinister grudge against us."

William, reluctantly, left the bedroom. He found Wren and Robin Erco—Lady Robin herself—peeking in each bedroom on the second floor using flashlights they'd brought with them.

"Wren," William said, trying not to seem disappointed to see her. He wasn't disappointed, exactly. He loved Wren. He'd never loved anyone like he loved her, but they hadn't been able to make a romance work with each other. Their platonic love had not crossed into romantic, no matter how hard they'd tried to fit it in that box. Their love was just not the right shape for the romance box.

"Willie!" Wren jumped at him, pulling him into a huge hug and bonking him on the back of the head with her flashlight. "Surprise!"

"Yeah. It is. Hi, Robin." Robin leaned against a doorframe and waved. "Nice jacket," he said. She was wearing a black leather jacket with lots of zippers.

"You flirt," Robin drawled, and William's face flushed. Robin kind of had that effect on everyone. She was effortlessly cool.

"What have you been up to?" Wren asked. "Were you asleep? It's only nine o'clock."

"Not much else to do here with no power, but no, I wasn't asleep. Why'd you guys come early? This morning you said you'd wait until tomorrow."

William led them back down the stairs and into the kitchen. No reason to stand around on the landing.

"I felt bad about you being stuck here alone, especially considering we rarely see you anymore. I was worried you'd spend tonight working." Wren was being a chatterbox, as always.

Robin laughed, low and husky. "He's not alone." He snapped his gaze to her, and she shrugged. "Benji Holiday's monster truck is out there."

"Monster truck?" William hadn't noticed Benji's vehicle the few times he'd opened the door today. Benji owning a monster truck was not that surprising. He was delightfully weird.

"It's not a monster. It's a 1980 Ford F-150 Ranger XLT four-by-four short bed." The three of them whipped around at Benji's voice. Benji had thrown on baggy sweats and his orange poncho. He smiled shyly. "Hi."

William couldn't hold in a starry-eyed grin.

Wren, thank God, was not looking at him. Robin was.

"Benji didn't get the memo about the postponement of the party. He got here around lunch," William explained.

"Oh, that sucks, Benji," Wren said. "You must have been bored all day. Especially with this one." She flicked her thumb at William, but before anyone could respond, she said, "We need beer. I had the longest day."

"We left it in the car," Robin said. "Need to get our bags too. I'll help you carry everything in."

Robin waved William away when he made toward the door to help them. Once the door closed behind them,

Benji puffed out his cheeks and let out a big breath. "So, Robin can tell."

William laughed. "Robin might just assume. Her parties are, well …" He stopped. He had no idea if Benji knew about Robin's parties. She kept them pretty secret.

"Have you been to Robin's orgies?"

Okay, he knew.

"A time or two. Have you?"

"Robin sees me as a little brother. No one invites their little brother to an orgy." Benji's eyes went wide. "Oh God, please tell me you haven't fucked my sister. Or my soon-to-be brother-in-law. I know they go to those parties, and I'm not sure I can handle that."

"No. Anyway, I haven't gone to one in years. Way before Perry was on the scene." No reason to tell Benji that the only person he'd ever slept with at a Lady Robin's orgy was Wren. Well, actually, maybe he *should* explain that to Benji.

"Whew. That's good. I mean, I say I couldn't handle it, but also …" He shrugged. "I like you. So I could probably put it from my brain momentarily while you put your tongue in my—"

The front door banged open, and Wren and Robin stomped in. They both looked like rockstars—Wren a goth goddess with pale skin and ripped clothes, Robin all steampunk and femme fatale.

"It's sleeting out there. Sleet is the worst type of precipitation. Like, make up your mind, sleet! Are you rain or are you snow?" Wren set down a duffle bag and case of beer before tugging her shoes off. "Beers all around."

William got the fire going again, since it didn't seem as if Wren and Robin were planning to head to bed soon. Benji split the gas station brownie into four parts, which William thought was very gracious of him, and passed a square to everyone. Robin and Wren settled on the couch together. Benji plopped down on the rug again, which made William flashback to their afternoon exertions in that very spot. Benji grinned at him.

William sat in the chair.

From there, he'd have a perfect view of Benji without it being obvious that he was staring at him. William could be contemplating the fire. No one would be any wiser.

"Willie, how did your date go last week?" Wren asked. She turned to Benji. "William's New Year's resolution was to find love."

William tensed. Benji tensed.

"Don't call me that, Wren, and it wasn't to find love. It was to go on some dates."

"Whatever." Wren waved her hand and grinned. "So how was it, lover boy?"

"It was not great."

"What happened?" she asked.

"She was a teetotaler. Didn't like my job. The meal turned into a lecture." William took a sip of beer to put an extra-fine point on it.

Wren sighed sadly. "What about the date with Dray?"

William tried not to glare at her. The last thing he

wanted to do was hash out his disastrous first dates in front of Benji.

"When you set me up with Dray, dear friend, you forgot to mention that they're still in love with their ex. We got drunk and went bowling. It was fun. We'll do it again soon. *Not as a date* because they're *in love with their ex.*"

That had been William's most successful date since he'd started this whole relationship search, which was telling. William chanced a glance at Benji. He was watching the exchange avidly.

"Oh, shoot," Wren said. "I was worried about that. Well, there are plenty of fish and all that. Did you at least make a list of—"

"I don't want to talk about my love life," William said, cutting her off before she could mention his list. God, he hadn't thought about his list of criteria since Benji had barreled in.

Robin ran her fingers through Wren's hair. "Give it a rest, babe. No one enjoys being put on the spot about being single on Valentine's Day."

Wren slumped. "Fine."

Now that William was interested in dating again, Wren had taken it as her God-given duty to find him someone. He secretly thought she might carry guilt around that they hadn't been able to make their relationship work all those years ago. Sometimes, he felt a bit of guilt about it too.

He watched Wren eat her brownie and sip from her can of Bud Light. No matter how much money she made, no matter how many successful lines of lingerie she created, she would always carry a piece of that girl from the trailer park with her. Seeing her with a can of cheap beer and black jeans and a distressed T-shirt—strategically shredded to show off very exceptional lace underneath—brought him right back to being teenagers with her and sitting on a lawn chair outside her house.

He knew she'd always have that trailer park inside her because he'd always have it inside of him too.

"If you won't regale us with dating horror stories, the least you can do is entertain us with work stories," Wren said. "I've already made Robin tell me her funny work stories. They got a shipment of new butt plugs today. The plugs have emojis on the base. She gave me a heart-eyes one."

"They're in beta test," Robin said. "I'm not sure we'll follow through with this idea."

"Can you beat butt plugs, William?" Benji asked, a teasing lilt to his voice.

"Doubt it." William thought for a few seconds. His job seemed glamorous—owning nightclubs—but mostly, he was a numbers guy. His business partner, Tina, handled more of the day-to-day management stuff. "I'm responsible for finding five bachelorians for our Bach Auction at Mount next weekend. We had several drop out this week. They evidently found love right before Valentine's Day. If you are aware of any single people who'd be willing to donate some kind of good or service, let me know."

"What's a bachelorian? Sounds like something out of *Star Trek*," Benji said.

"That's why I like it." William smiled at him. "It's the word the manager of Mount came up with to replace bachelor or bachelorette."

"How do you plan to find five bachelorians on short notice?" Robin asked.

"We have a handful of late applications I can dig through, but Tina told me to hit up friends too. So, Wren? Want to be in the Bach Auction? The proceeds go to SAFE Asylum."

Robin glanced slyly at Wren. "Aren't you dating that bartender?"

William sat up abruptly. "You're dating someone?" Normally, Wren kept him in the loop on that stuff.

Wren shrugged. "I'm not dating Marina. I've had a few trysts with Marina and her wife, Leslie."

Trysts. That was an interesting word. Was that what he and Benji were doing? Having a tryst?

A Valentine's Day tryst.

Do not look at Benji. Do not gaze longingly at Benji.

"I'd be happy to be one of your bachelorians. Do I have to actually go on a date?" Wren asked in a way that indicated "a date" was the worst thing in the entire world.

"Of course not. You'll get a drink token to spend on your highest bidder, but other than that, all you'll need to do is arrange to deliver whatever good or service you're providing."

"Could I offer like a customized lingerie consultation and product creation?"

The actual value of that from Wren would be quite high. He'd owe her big time.

"If you're offering that, I'll be there with bells on and a full fucking wallet," Benji said. "Shit. I shouldn't have bought that Valentine's Day candy. Oh well. I'll redo my budget." He said the last part as if he were talking only to himself.

A surprised silence followed Benji's words. Benji's cheeks darkened, and he laughed self-consciously. A weird combination of heat and tenderness flared through William.

"Aren't you a wonder," Wren said softly. William could tell that Wren was taking Benji's measure, thinking up designs in her head.

"Benji, you're single, right?" Robin asked.

William's stomach jumped.

Benji tossed a glance toward William. "R-right. Yes."

"There you go, William. A hot, gay, single twenty-four-year-old with a very marketable skillset." Robin grinned slowly, a cat-who-got-the-canary glint in her eyes.

"What's my marketable skillset?" Benji asked, his voice wooden.

"Car stuff, obviously," Robin said. "An oil change or a car detailing."

Benji scoffed. "Changing your oil is easy. No one would bid on that."

"Uh, I would," William said. "I have no idea how to change the oil in my ego machine out there."

"You could watch a YouTube video."

William scowled. "Don't sell yourself short." Then

William scowled deeper. He should shut up. He didn't exactly like the idea of Benji being part of the Bach Auction, though dates weren't expected. It was basically a romance novel waiting to happen. Benji would probably meet a cowboy billionaire there, then one thing would lead to another and there would only be *one bed*!

"Okay," Benji said with a smile. "I'm in. It's a good cause."

"There you go, William," Wren said. "Two bachelorians. Now you only need three. Robin, you in?"

"No."

Everyone laughed except for Robin, who smiled archly. Her dark tan skin was sparkly along her cheekbones—highlighter, William's brain provided helpfully, though he had no idea where he'd picked up that info—and she had on plum-colored lipstick. He'd known Robin for years, but she'd always been reserved. Some people thought she was cold, but that wasn't true. She was commanding and watchful. The first to jump in with a telling insight or a witticism. The first to notice when something was off.

Therefore, she was the last person he expected to pull a book of Mad Libs out of her purse and say, "We did a Valentine's Day popup shop last week, and one of our products is this book of sexy Mad Libs. The scenes were crafted by top erotica writers. Wanna play?"

The four of them had nothing better to do and could have done a lot worse in the entertainment department. At least the topic was no longer William's love life.

Wren tried to use a close variant or synonym of spurt for every verb: splurt, squirt, splooge, emit, spray, release.

Benji was on a roll with his adjectives: meaty, slippery, forceful, potent, vigorous, virile, suckable.

Robin read each Mad Libs back to them in the driest, most serious voice.

It took William a few minutes to figure out why the Mad Libs were turning him on so much. During the last Mad Lib, he was sitting there, trying to hide his giant hard-on when Benji glanced at him shyly through his gold-tipped eyelashes and said, "Needy." Then, "Dominating." And lastly, "Full."

And everything became quite clear.

Chapter Ten

Benji finally gave up and called it a night. Wren seemed to have enough energy to stay up until morning, but Benji was hoping if he set an example of going to bed, everyone else would too.

He could only say "come fuck me" via adjectives in so many ways. His brain was starting to hurt. As was his dick.

As he trudged up the stairs, Benji heard William address room logistics with Robin and Wren. Benji hoped that William would finagle it in a way that made it easy for him to sneak to the top floor. And if William did show up, Benji was going to be prepared.

Super prepared.

He took a fast shower in a pitch-black bathroom, put the garter belt and stockings back on (because, hello, he looked hot in them), brushed his teeth, made sure all the toys were clean, rescattered the rose petals, relit the candles in the room, and picked some lint off a dildo.

Still no William.

Benji opened his phone. Half-past eleven. And only five percent battery. Damn.

Benji started making deals with himself.

If William didn't show by 11:35 p.m., he'd eat a piece of Valentine's Day candy and go to sleep.

If William didn't show by 11:40 p.m., he'd drink the sparkling cider he'd smuggled up here and eat two pieces of Valentine's Day candy. Then straight to bed.

If William didn't show up by 11:45 p.m., he'd jerk off.

If William didn't show up by midnight, he'd allow himself to come.

The door creaked open at 11:58 p.m., and William stuck his head into the room, as if he were scared of waking Benji up.

He didn't wake Benji up. Benji was already *up*. William banged his head into the doorframe. Then he banged the door into his knee as he hurriedly shut it behind him.

If William was trying to sneak in quietly, he'd failed.

Benji could imagine the sight he presented, laying on his back facing the door. Fucking himself with the Swamp Monster Everglides Dildo. A few strokes of his fist away from coming.

"You took a long time," Benji panted. "Wasn't sure you were coming."

"Hold up." William's voice was guttural and harsh.

Benji held up because he was nothing if not willing to follow William's every whim.

William tore his sweatshirt over his head and shucked

his flannel pajama bottoms off, leaving himself in nothing but those fuck-hot tighty-whities. Then he crawled onto the bed and kneeled beside Benji. Almost absently, William trailed a rose petal along Benji's ribs, right above the top of the garter belt.

"Beautiful. In this. Beautiful all the time. But damn, *in this*," William said. "Keep going. Let me watch you."

Benji was all arms, what with one hand on his cock, one on the dildo up his ass, his legs bent awkwardly so he could reach, but he also felt sexier than he'd ever felt in his entire life.

William moved that rose petal along Benji's collarbone, and the muscles in Benji's groin tightened, as if they were attached to this weird bone in his chest. Fucking fuck, William was teaching him new things about his body. Evidently every part of him was an erogenous zone if it was lightly grazed by a fucking rose petal.

Romance, man.

"I'm sorry it took me so long," William whispered. "I didn't mean to leave you hanging."

"You didn't." Benji's eyes rolled back in his head, and he had to let his cock go for a second. Having William in the room, watching him—Benji really liked being watched, being on display, being photographed—well, it ratcheted up the intensity of everything, especially the punch against his prostate, which honestly, had already been overwhelming pre-William. Once he wasn't a breath away from coming, Benji said, "Glad I waited for you, though."

William caught Benji's hand, the hand that had just

left his cock, and brought it up to his lips, pressing a kiss to the palm. Even that, even a tiny kiss on his hand, made his stomach flutter.

"Me too." William gently lifted Benji's arm above his head. The rose petal in his hand had gone floppy from handling, so he picked up another.

The feathery light tickle of the petal down his triceps had Benji twisting and an odd whining noise slipping from his mouth.

"Okay?" William asked.

"Uh-huh." Benji was so focused on the simple touch of the petal as it travelled over the tendon of his armpit that he stopped fucking himself. "You have a thing for armpits," he was able to say as William brushed the rose petal back up Benji's arm.

"Yes. Sorry. I can stop." William's gaze was riveted to Benji's face.

"It's okay. I think I like it, but want … I don't know."

More, more.

Benji stared up into William's eyes, and William didn't blink as he leaned down and kissed the soft skin below Benji's pit hair.

Benji moaned. Loud.

"Please, William."

"Yes, baby. I've got you."

Before the tingles from being called "baby" had fully traversed Benji's body, William licked up the same tendon he'd caressed with the rose petal.

Heat blasted through Benji. He writhed. He cried out. Pre-come dribbled down his cock.

Benji jerked his hand back to his dick. God, he couldn't not touch himself after that.

"Fuck yourself harder, sweetheart. Want to watch you shoot." William stretched out next to him, holding himself up on one elbow.

Benji's vision went fuzzy, the candlelight in the room turning to yellow-orange blurs, but he tried to keep his eyes open as William lifted a rose petal to his lips.

It was … God, it was romantic. Yes, Benji was all arms, and he was fucking himself with a dildo he called Swampy. And it was cold in the bedroom. And he knew he needed to be quieter, but the kiss of a rose petal over his chin, over his cheekbone, and back to his bottom lip was so incredibly sweet.

"That's it, Benji. So pretty."

That word. *Pretty*. Why did it affect him the way it did? Maybe he'd never know. Maybe it didn't matter.

Because he came, silently, staring up into William's deep brown eyes.

Reflexive tears leaked out of Benji's eyes, and he didn't hide them. He tried to tell himself that he wasn't hiding because this thing with William didn't count. They were secret fake valentines. They'd fuck all weekend, then move on. Benji would get to experience a bit of romance without pretending to be someone he wasn't. William would get some practice dating or what-the-fuck-ever. They didn't know each other and didn't really need to.

But Benji couldn't deny that this was how sex was *supposed* to feel. This was how sex felt when *no one* was hiding. When the vulnerability of it was honored and both parties entered into it with joy and honesty.

When it was real.

William got off the bed, taking the dildo with him. Benji could hear the sink running in the bathroom before William returned with a warm, wet rag. William kissed Benji's temple, catching a tear track, but didn't say anything. Then he dashed the washrag over Benji's cheeks and under his nose, which made Benji laugh wetly. He hadn't been getting snot anywhere, but he was leaking tears, so it wasn't an unusual assumption.

William flipped the rag over and blotted a come spot on the garter belt, his brow furrowing in concentration. His glasses were slightly askew, and his hair was chaotic in the front. Benji surely looked like an even bigger mess.

"I washed your dildo," William whispered.

"A man after my own heart." Benji's voice was scratchy, and he had to laugh at himself again. His emotions were the worst—and the best—because he wouldn't trade anything for the way his heart flipped when William smiled at him.

"Are you okay?" William asked.

"Yeah. I think so."

"Good. Turn over for me. Spoiling time isn't over."

Benji was helpless to resist. He liked being spoiled. He especially liked being spoiled by William.

William dribbled lube over his fingers and gently pressed them into Benji, but once he was there, he didn't escalate it. He used his free hand to rub over Benji's back and shoulders and legs, petting him all over.

"Still good?" William asked.

Benji nodded and rested his head in his arms. He loved ass play, but to lie here, after he had come, and let William keep him stretched and full was a totally new experience. It probably wouldn't take too long to get Benji going, not with William stroking his prostate gently again and again.

But not yet. Right now, he was happy to lie back and bask.

"I've been thinking about why I'm so into lingerie," Benji said.

William leaned in and kissed Benji's neck. "Tell me."

"I've always felt kind of confined by expectations. Going back"—Benji blew out a big breath—"fuck, going back to when I was very young. My parents basically bailed after I was born, and it's never stopped hurting, you know?"

"I can imagine." William started to pull his fingers out, then paused. "Want me to stop fingering you so we can talk? I can't tell if this is an acceptable-while-getting-fingered topic."

"Don't stop. I'm all floaty and wanna chat."

"Okay. I won't."

"Anyway, my parents wanted me to be different than I was. On the handful of occasions one or both showed up, they acted like I was a bit too soft for them. So I tried to be who they wanted me to be."

"How young were you?"

"Oh geez, early elementary the first time I truly clocked it. I was obsessed with unicorns. I had them on everything—backpack, folders, pencil box. My dad said something shitty, so I asked my grandma to replace them. She wouldn't. We didn't have the money to buy new stuff. Rosie traded me and took the unicorn stuff to middle school."

"I hate that they made you feel that way."

Benji shrugged. "Yeah. Me too. Then, as a teenager, I hid behind this mask of disinterest. I was the emo gay guy with lots of emo friends, but I wasn't open with who I was in my heart. I didn't laugh loudly or share my thoughts. I used sarcasm and *cattiness* to hide. I dyed my hair black and wore eyeliner and band T-shirts. I never sang or danced."

"Are you a good singer and dancer?" William asked, surprised, like maybe he thought Benji was harboring secret dreams of Broadway.

"No, I'm horrible, but I can murder me some karaoke."

"What happened when you got older? You're not an emo boy anymore."

"No. It got worse. I shape-shifted into what I thought was a dateable, fuckable gay man. I compromised. I changed myself to be the guy each new asshole wanted me to be until I was a total blank slate inside. I'd penned myself into this sanitized acceptability except when I was with my sisters, where I could be myself. The lingerie is a big fuck you to that. I'm not that person. I'm *this* person. And yes, I like that my legs look jacked in thigh-highs, *and*

I can change a tire faster than anyone around. I like to cuddle, *and* I can tell you every player on the Royals roster. I like unicorns, *and* I can still, I don't know, top like a machine if the mood hits. I like to wear pretty things, but that doesn't make me less than. It makes me the person I want to be. I can be more than one thing."

A heavy silence followed Benji's words, so he glanced back at William. William was considering him seriously.

"I don't think I'd want you to top me like a machine. I'd want you to top me like a living, breathing human. You're beautiful and amazing, and I'm so thankful I've met this version of you. The real one. I only want you to be the real you with me."

This was evidently a weekend of romantic list-toppers because that might have been the most romantic thing anyone had ever said to Benji. But his brain caught on two sentences in particular.

"You want me to fuck you?"

"The thought of you fucking me while wearing this … damn, I love that."

"But I thought you liked giving me directions and being in control."

"No reason I can't be in control when you fuck me, honey, but only if you want it."

Benji wanted it. His body was lighting back up.

"Yeah. Okay. Now?"

"Do you want it to be now? We can keep talking."

"No talking. Now."

"Think you need something inside you first," William said gruffly. "Pick." He grabbed a few of the toys that were on the other side of the bed and sat them in Benji's line of vision.

The P-Spot Pulse—a prostate massager.

A string of anal beads.

A silicone cock ring attached to a Rimmy butt plug.

He wanted to feel full, so he pointed at the cock ring and plug. He'd never worn it while fucking someone, just while jerking off. He rolled onto his back.

"I think you'll need to put this part on yourself," William said, handing him the ring.

Benji spread lube on the inside of the ring, before wrapping it around his balls and cock, thankful he wasn't fully hard yet. It boned him right up though. The condom quickly followed.

The plug was connected to the cock ring via a longish silicone cord, which gave the user a lot of slack and room to maneuver.

"Do you need more prep to get this in?" William asked. He grabbed the lube.

"No. I'm ready."

The plug was not an easy fit. The bulb was a stretch, but Benji had played with it enough to know how to take it. His stomach was fluttery with anticipation, and if he clenched, the heavy plug would rub against his prostate.

"What does this button do?" William asked, touching the raised button on the base of the plug.

"Press it."

William did. A faint vibrating noise filled the room. The sensation sent shivery pleasure up Benji's spine, and his knees immediately went weak and shaky.

"It's called the Rimmy," Benji said. "There are tiny nodules that rotate around the neck to simulate getting rimmed. It's fabulous. Almost as amazing as actually getting rimmed."

"Fuck. Okay. That's really sexy. Knowing you're feeling that right now."

They traded places—William on his back and Benji kneeling between his legs.

"Do you want to take your glasses off?" Benji asked him.

William's eyes were wide and full of intensity. He shook his head. "Want to be able to see you."

It went quickly from there, William ordering Benji to work two fingers in. Then three. At last, William said, "Get in me, sweetheart. Go slow. It's been awhile."

"How long is awhile?" Benji asked. He gripped the back of William's thighs and pushed them toward his chest. The nylon of Benji's stockings rubbed the back of William's legs, which Benji enjoyed. He wiggled to feel it more.

"Ah, over a year?"

"Since you've fucked yourself or since you've been fucked by someone else."

"Myself."

Benji positioned himself at William's entrance. "How long since you've been fucked by someone else?"

William's head dropped back, exposing the long line of his neck. He had a small tuft of hair below the base of his throat that Benji was definitely going to lick soon. Benji loved a nice hairy chest.

"Three years?" William said, like he wasn't sure. "Her name was Evangelina. Can't remember the exact date. Need me to find the calendar, or are you gonna fuck me?"

Benji was nothing if not obliging. He was going to be the best valentine ever.

William made the most fantastic noise as Benji pushed in. A rumbly mix between a moan, a growl, and a sigh. It was loud. The combination of the plug in Benji's ass, the cock ring lifting his balls and hardening him, and the tight squeeze of William's hole caused Benji to make an equally needy sound.

If they weren't careful, they'd wake Wren and Robin, and their secret fake valentines gig would be up.

Benji smothered his next noise in William's calf. William's eyes were closed and his brow furrowed. He looked to be in pain, but his gorgeous cock was rock hard, the head peeking through foreskin.

"You good, William?"

William nodded and gasped as that last barrier inside him seemed to ease, and Benji bottomed out.

Once they both recovered from how wonderful it felt, William gritted out, "Put your hands on the headboard. Stretch out over me."

Their difference in height allowed Benji to reach the headboard by curling William's lower half slightly off the bed. The candlelight from the side table closest to them painted William's pale skin in gold. Rose petals were rumpled under their bodies.

Benji stared straight down into William's eyes and

moved in him. With him. William curled his fingers into the garter belt and held on.

"How does it feel to fuck me while wearing something lacy? You like it?" William asked.

His questions slammed Benji's awareness back into his body. He'd been floating on general nice sensations, but suddenly, he was overwhelmed by the way the garters pulled at his stockings each time he thrust. The lace wrapping his torso was slightly scratchy against his skin. The nylon of the thigh-highs shifted against the soles of his feet.

"I feel sexy."

"Yeah," William panted, gripping Benji's sides harder. "You are, baby. And the cock ring?"

"Makes my dick so thick, and everything is more intense. I'm more sensitive."

"What about the plug?" As William said this, he locked his legs around the back of Benji's thighs, forcing their bodies closer together. The slight change in angle pressed said plug into Benji's hot spot.

"Oh God, can't talk." The jolt to his system made him move a little rougher than before.

William's eyes went hazy and his breath thundered out of him, a flush coloring his neck and chest. His body was slick with sweat. "That's it. Make me love it, sweetheart," he gasped. "You make me love it."

They twisted together for long minutes, their bodies dancing and responding in sync. William's dirty words and bossiness dropped off into deep, dark sounds in the back of his throat.

Benji fell to his elbows on top of William, wanting to be as close as humanly possible. William held him tenderly, adoringly, like Benji was precious.

There were so many things Benji wanted to do. He wanted to hold William down and really fuck him. He wanted to suck hickeys along William's collarbones, to stake a claim. He wanted to lick William's armpit and see if it made him bust.

But this was too good to stop. This closeness. This connectedness.

Next time. He'd do those things next time.

God, let there be a next time. Let this be more than a passing fancy, more than drowning their Valentine's Day loneliness in each other.

Benji's heartbeat slammed in time with William's, like William's heart was a metronome that Benji's couldn't help but match.

William lifted his head up to capture Benji's mouth, and that was all it took. Benji loudly moaned his orgasm out against William's lips. Secrecy be damned.

Benji drowned in it, the normal tension and release amplified and prolonged until he was weak and wobbly and exposed.

William's words slowly reached Benji's ears.

"I've got you. I've got you. So hot."

Benji whimpered. It was too much. Too many revelations in his head. His heart.

Too much.

Benji lifted up but didn't pull out. He was still hard because the cock ring was preventing him from going soft as quickly as usual. The skin of his cock was tingling and sensitive. The Rimmy was continuing to work its magic, making him twitch and shiver. He felt like a live wire.

He reached between them to jerk William's dick, and William shouted. A spurt of pre-come dribbled down William's cock, catching momentarily on his retracted foreskin before dripping onto his stomach and glossing his already sweat-slick skin. Benji could have watched that image on a loop for hours.

"Keep fucking me. Make me come," William groaned. His voice wasn't bossy or demanding but tortured. Tortured was beautiful on him. "Oh God. *Benji*. Make me come."

Benji fisted William's prick and thrust into him hard. William's eyes rolled back. It only took a few slow strokes for William's penis to throb in Benji's hand and for spunk to jet out in perfect pulses all over William's chest, neck, and holy hell, his chin.

Afterward, they stared at each other, perhaps both a little shocked. Then a laugh cracked through William. He touched his chin before looking at his sticky fingers. William laughed again and said, "What the fuck?"

Chapter Eleven

William had never shot like that. He could taste come on his lips.

He should get fucked more often. Damn. Maybe he'd add that to his list of dating criteria.

Must be open to fucking me.

Must have beautiful big blue eyes.

Must be named Benji freaking Holiday because wow.

Benji finally pulled out—he was still sporting a semi since sex toys were evidently magic—and went about removing all his implements and the condom. He seemed to be concentrating on it really hard, not even throwing a glance at William before hurrying off to the bathroom to clean up.

William wanted to sit up, but he was a mess. He was worried about getting come everywhere. A thin tremble of uneasiness went through him. Benji had left, and William wasn't sure if Benji was washing up or if he was hiding.

"Umm, Benji?" he whispered, his voice very loud in the silent bedroom.

Benji popped his head out from the en suite bathroom. "Yeah?"

"Are we okay?" William hated how hesitant he sounded. He'd hoped getting older would make him bolder when it came to sex, but Benji made him feel young again—in the best and, also, worst ways.

"Sure." Whatever Benji saw in William made his expression soften. "I'll be there in a second to clean you up."

"Okay." William let out an unsteady breath.

Something inside him had shifted, and it wasn't because of the very special dicking out he'd just received. His heart was pounding hard, and he was struggling not to let his emotions go flying.

He was happy and so terrified that Benji wasn't.

Benji returned with a damp cloth and very efficiently cleaned William up. It was nice to be taken care of.

He was the master of his own closed-off universe most of the time. Wren tried to baby him occasionally, like when he was sick or stressed, but he never let her. He didn't want to admit why he usually rejected caretaking, as well as the simple attention Benji was bestowing upon him now, but he couldn't hide from himself forever.

It felt good.

It felt so good that he didn't think he'd ever want to give it up. It felt like an indulgence, and he'd never allowed time in his life for indulgences. He was worried he'd come to depend on it, to need it. And fuck, but Benji was definitely going to rip this away from him one day. Soon. Like, Sunday soon.

"You okay?" Benji asked him eventually, after William curled to hide his face against Benji's side.

William nodded.

"Who's showing up tomorrow?" Benji asked.

"The usual crew, minus Rosie. She hasn't come to this thing since before the divorce."

Benji hummed. "I didn't know Rosie and Voldemort had been regular attendees of this," Benji said, referring to his oldest sister and her cheating ex. William happened to think Voldemort was a fairly apt assessment of Rosie's ex, except Voldemort had more personality. "No one had ever told me anything about this party," Benji continued. "Is it like Fight Club?"

Laughter bubbled up through William. He pressed it into Benji's skin.

"It's not. I figured you knew about it. This is our seventh year, I think. The third here at my house. The originals were me, Wren, Robin, Sasha, Rosie, and Avi. Tomorrow, Avi and his husband, Manuel, plus Sasha and Perry will arrive. It'll be a full house."

"Where will you sleep?"

William's stomach flopped. Was that a hint? Did Benji want him to sleep elsewhere tonight?

"I planned to sleep in the sunroom," William said, as neutrally as possible. "I have a space heater and an air mattress ready to go."

Benji didn't seem to have anything to say to that, but his body went spiky against William, as if he'd stopped relaxing, all elbows and knees. He sat up and unclipped the garters from his stockings and rolled the nylons down his legs gently. When he reached back to get at the hook-and-eye enclosures of the garter belt, William stopped him.

"Let me."

"All right," Benji said.

William kneeled behind Benji and kissed the back of his neck. "Benji," he murmured. He slowly unclasped each fastener on the belt. "I'll be honest, I'm feeling a bit shaky. I—"

Benji turned in his arms like a wild thing—fast and agile and fierce. Benji took the belt from William and tossed it off the bed. "You're a big softie, huh? You take care of business in every aspect of your life but never let anyone return the favor."

It was so close to William's thinking earlier that he reeled back.

Benji wasn't done. "You spoil me, but I bet my ass you're uncomfortable getting spoiled back."

"I certainly feel off-kilter."

Benji kissed him, and some of the weird tension between them eased. William sighed, and Benji relaxed in his arms.

"Can you blow out the candles?" Benji asked when they came up for air. "I'll rid the bed of rose petals and sex toys."

"I can stay?"

Benji blinked. "If you want to."

"I do."

William liked having a plan. After taking care of the candles, petals, sex toys, and stoking the fire, they finished getting ready for bed. Benji put a pair of silk boxers on under his silky T-shirt, and William donned his flannel pajama bottoms.

They found each other in the middle of the bed, and William almost immediately started to drop off to sleep.

"We're great at sex," Benji whispered baldly.

"Yeah."

"It's not been that good for me before."

William woke back up. "Me either," he admitted.

"I think your house is haunted. By sex fairies. Or horny little cupids. There's no reason it should be this good."

William could think of one very good reason, but he wasn't brave enough to look it in the face.

Instead, he said, "Valentine's Day mojo. We have it."

"Will we have it tomorrow?" The rest of Benji's question went unspoken, but William could read between the lines. *Will this continue tomorrow when there are more people to hide from? When my sister is here?*

"If you want us to." The rest of William's statement went unspoken too. *Do you want us to?*

William woke up at five the next morning. He always woke up at five. His body's internal clock liked routine, but this morning he would have loved a few extra hours of blissful sleep with Benji.

Ah well. To keep this a secret, he had to sneak out early anyway. Robin had insomnia, so they were at risk of being caught if she decided to start her morning rather than lie in bed awake. He needed to make it seem as if he'd slept on the couch in the living room. His plan had been to fill the air mattress in the sunroom last night, but his emotions after Benji fucked him had totally waylaid him. He couldn't blow it up now—the portable air pump would be too loud.

Last night, he hadn't had his wits about him. All he'd cared about was getting back to Benji. Wren had wanted to chat as he'd gotten her set up on the futon in his office.

He'd been so focused on his plan to slip back into Benji's room he'd missed the fact that Wren had found his handwritten dating profile and criteria.

He'd just finished tucking a fresh sheet around the futon mattress when Wren had said, "You need to add something on here about being a great cook. You suck at cooking. You should try to bag an amateur chef."

William had whipped around. "Hey! Privacy."

Wren had glanced up from the paper in surprise. To be fair, creating the dating criteria had been her idea, and he'd planned to talk to her about it this weekend.

Then Benji had shown up.

"Well, sorry." She'd put the papers on the desk, and William had sighed.

"Being able to cook would be a plus, but not sure it's a deal-breaker," he'd said.

She'd smiled. "You're telling me that if someone

doesn't like true crime, that *would be* a deal breaker for you?"

He'd flushed. "This whole thing is dumb. It's not as easy as bullet points on a piece of copy paper. I don't know the first thing about finding love. Don't have any idea what would make a person compatible with me."

"Of course you do, but you're being stubbornly boring about it." She'd waved toward the papers like they were Exhibit A. "Go to bed, Willie. We'll talk tomorrow."

"Fine," he'd grumbled. "'Night." He'd kissed her cheek and escaped.

Was he being stubborn about finding the right person for him? Was it really so easy as writing down stipulations and personality traits on a piece of paper?

He turned his head toward Benji, studying the delicate cusp of his earlobe, the gentle slope of his jaw, the pointy knob at the top of his spine.

Nothing was so simple anymore. The man in William's arms was better than any criteria he could dream up.

He tried to slip away from Benji. They'd migrated in the night until Benji's back was curled against William's side. As soon as William started to move, Benji flopped over and flung an arm across William's waist.

"No," Benji murmured.

"No, what?"

"Leaving." Benji pressed a sleepy kiss to William's shoulder, and William's entire chest cavity melted with ooey-gooey feelings. He wished it weren't dark in the room. He wanted to get to experience morning Benji in full color and light.

He'd let Benji sleep for a bit longer. A few minutes wouldn't hurt. Benji hooked his leg over William's thigh, effectively holding him hostage.

Cuddle hostage. Oh geez, this was even better than the couch. William trailed his fingers down Benji's forearm and back up to his bicep. His arms were cut, the muscles bulgy and defined. He probably had to lift heavy stuff at his job. William loved the way Benji looked in silk and lace, but he was pretty intrigued by the thought of Benji in coveralls as well.

Benji's fingers twitched and tightened on William's chest, and he nudged his head in closer, forcing William to lift his arm and wrap it over Benji's shoulder.

Benji's leg went heavy against William, like he'd fallen back asleep, so William started contemplating his day. He had to call the electric company to see when the power would come back on today. If he got power back, he needed to find three more bachelorians for the auction. If he didn't get power, he might need to consider buying a generator. This afternoon, Sasha, Perry, Avi, and Manny would arrive, and tonight, they'd likely play a game, and if it wasn't sleeting, have a bonfire.

William's main objective today, though, was to figure out how to spend alone-time with Benji. To get Benji to view William as a viable option for after Valentine's Day. William closed his eyes. It could happen.

He could almost imagine it happening.

A warm, wet mouth suddenly sucked on the tendon

of his armpit, and William about flew out of his skin. His morning wood had mostly dissipated by that point, but it was back with a vengeance.

Benji lifted his head with a lazy smile. "Hi. I think I might be into this armpit thing. Let's dry hump and then watch the sunrise."

William's only response was a kiss.

Chapter Twelve

They watched the sunrise from the edge of the dock, sitting close in the chilly morning. But not close enough. Benji kept blowing breaths to see the ice crystals in the air, which was fun in a childlike way, but he'd much rather be able to climb into William's lap for warmth. To blow his breath against William's skin.

Too bad Wren and Robin, if they woke up, would be able to see them through the window, so Benji had to keep his hands to himself.

Benji felt mushy and half-formed this morning. He wasn't used to being awake so early. Maybe that was the cause of his unsteadiness. He definitely wasn't used to being awake this early without the aid of coffee. Or it could be that he was sure he'd die if he didn't get to lick the little divot at the join of William's jaw and neck. It was muddling him up.

The sun crested the tree line across the lake and Benji's breath caught.

"Worth it," he mumbled.

"What is?" William asked.

"Freezing my badonkadonk off to sit out here with you. Sunrises, man. Worth it."

"What about sunsets? We could watch it tonight."

"Sunrise … sunset." Benji hummed the song from *Fiddler on the Roof*, which made William stare at him with a bit of wonder in his eyes.

No one had ever looked at Benji the way William did. He didn't trust it. Yet. But it was nice—an ego boost—to have someone as fab as William gazing at him like that.

Was that all this was? An ego boost? A nice interlude to help Benji gain some confidence?

Was it the end of the world if it was? Maybe this was like the bridge of a song, short and special. The best part but over too fast. He stopped humming.

Fuck. Now Benji was writing poetry in his head over William O'Dare.

"Need coffee. And to charge my phone. Can we take your car to Starbucks?" Benji asked, interrupting the moment.

William laughed. "We can drive to the gas station, get to really experience all that the Kum & Go has to offer: pizza, brownie, coffee. You can charge your phone in my car."

"The gas station is not called Kum & Go."

"It is, and it's spelled K-U-M."

"Shut up!"

"Okay."

"No, don't actually shut up. I like your voice," Benji said.

William let loose a shy, happy grin. Benji watched the sunrise in William's eyes—the light reflecting off the lenses of his glasses and the sun a spark in his dark pupils.

The last day had presented so many things Benji had never done before: watched a sunrise with a lover, fucked on a bed of flower petals, made love in candlelight. It was a Valentine's Day crash course. Maybe that was why this was so intense between them. They'd been dressing it up with romantic fixings, like an amorous baked potato. But what if all they had was butter and chives? Would this be jumbling Benji's brain if they hadn't been pretending to be valentines? Would he feel like he was very quickly falling for this man if they didn't have these accouterments screaming *romance me, bitch*?

What would happen when it was just Benji and William—no rose petals, no candlelight, no winter sunrise? Just them. Would Benji still have this weird unnamable energy pinging around his stomach?

William scooted a bit closer, eliminating the space between their hips and shoulders. Then, with their backs to the lake house, William took Benji's hand in his, sending a zing up Benji's arm. William studied Benji's fingers for long seconds, examining each knuckle and nail like it was special.

Holding hands was such a sweet way to start a morning. Second only to frotting. William's thumb swept up the back of Benji's hand and over his knuckles. Their fingers were cold but quickly warmed from touching. Everything felt exaggerated to Benji, like he could discern each ridge and bump and groove of William's thumbprint as if it were etched into his own skin. He wanted that thumb on his Adam's apple, on his cheek, holding him steady and secure.

"You know, *rut* and *groove* are synonyms," Benji said into the charged silence between them.

William's lips tipped into that shiny, crooked smile. "I did know that."

"But if I said that I was 'in a rut,' that would be the exact opposite meaning of 'in a groove.'"

Benji wasn't sure why this point was so essential to make, but he liked the way his words lit up William's face.

"I'd never thought of that."

"Maybe you're not as smart as me," Benji said with a bit of a lilt.

"Probably true. I'm tired of being in a rut. Ready to get in a groove instead."

"Me too. Exactly."

William lifted his thumb to Benji's chin. Gah, this was all … a lot. He was feeling … a lot.

"Benji?"

"Yeah?"

"I don't want this to be fake. It's not fake to me."

Benji's heart slammed an uneven tattoo in his chest. He didn't want it to be fake either. He was tired of that excuse. He liked William. He really liked William, but it was scary.

"Cool. I agree." Benji had no idea what admitting

that meant. Did this make them not-fake valentines? Benji stood abruptly. "Coffee. Phone."

William peered up at him, looking (again!) like a model for WASPy pajamas, sitting temptingly on a wooden dock in the thin light of dawn.

Motherfucker.

He didn't wait to see if William followed him back into the house. William did.

Thirty minutes later, they were both showered (showering with only a kerosene lantern for light seemed very *Little House on the Prairie* to Benji—he was not a fan) and dressed and en route to coffee. Benji plugged his phone into a charger in William's dumb Alfa Romeo Giulia. It lit up with a handful of notifications, but he ignored them to open his photos from the night before.

Static filled his ears and blood rushed to his cheeks. The images were shadowy and dark, but the candlelight had sent licks of light over random parts of his body—the round jut of his hip, the arch of his foot, the point of his elbow. Benji's favorite was one with William's hand on his thigh under the garter. He never got pics this sexy and evocative on his own, and he had a whole backdrop and lighting setup.

"What do you think?" William asked.

William was driving, relaxed with one hand on the wheel and one on the gearshift. His ease with a car would normally turn Benji on and take his whole focus—he was a motorhead, after all—but he was too distracted by the images.

"They're hot." He was amazed and frustrated that

William had been able to take such good pictures with so little effort.

"Yeah, you are."

Benji snorted. "Thanks, booger bear."

"Oh God. Don't call me that. It's worse than Wren calling me Willie."

"I honestly disagree with that assessment. Willie is pretty bad," Benji said very solemnly.

William laughed, his face lighting up and the cutest crinkles forming on his nose. Benji wanted to kiss them. He refrained.

"Are you going to delete the pictures?" William asked.

"Nah. I'll add them to my secret Benji-in-sexy-under-things folder."

"You have a secret folder for that?"

"Yes."

"How many pictures are in it?"

Benji shrugged. "A bunch. Fifty maybe? I only keep my favorites."

They arrived at the gas station, which was, in fact, named Kum & Go. Benji's phone had only reached a twenty percent charge.

William turned in his seat to face Benji. William's color was high on his face, and his eyes were a bit wild. "What do you do with them?"

"Look at them."

"You don't show them to people?"

"No. Why would I?"

An almost feral smile tipped William's mouth.

"Because you're sexy. You don't think about showing that off?"

Benji's breath stalled out in his throat. His mouth went dry. It was like William could see right through him. "I do. I actually have a blank Instagram profile I created that's not associated with my name for that purpose."

"What's holding you back?"

"This feels like therapy," Benji joked. He didn't know what was holding him back. Maybe some misplaced fear about putting his body out there on the Internet. His grandma had once warned him that "the Internet is forever, and no one wants to see your dick, Benji." But his photos weren't nudes, and most of his favorite pics were safe for work. Or *just about* safe for work.

"Sorry," William said. "Mostly, I want to see them, so I'm trying to wrangle this conversation so you give me a glimpse."

"Oh. Here." Benji handed over his phone. "You can look."

William scrolled backward through the images, starting with the ones he'd taken last night. He lingered over one in which Benji was sporting a white, high-leg, wide-weave mesh brief.

"Oh, hon," William breathed, and a delicious ache spread through Benji, pulsing out of him from every pressure point, like one big nerve ending. William handed the phone back without thumbing through more photos. "Don't want to spoil it."

"Spoil what?"

"The surprise when they end up on your Instagram.

Because, Benji, those are amazing. If you want to share them with the world, you should. You could be a—what's it called?—an influencer? An Instagram model. An Insta-gay? That's art, baby."

"You're too old to say Instagay," Benji said. William, disappointingly, didn't take the bait. Benji glanced down at the phone. "You think?"

"Yes." William's voice was self-assured. It filled Benji with sudden confidence.

"This one first?" He held up his phone, flashing the pic of him in the white briefs. In the image, he was in profile, giving a perfect view of the high cut of the briefs' sides and a coy peek at the shape of his ass. He had his arm on the wall in front of him, partially obscuring his face.

"Oh. I mean, yeah. If you're sure. Don't let me pressure you."

"You're not." Benji sucked in a breath, opened the photo in his app, gave it a simple caption ("Getting cheeky") with the designer tagged and a few hashtags, then tapped on the share button. He let the breath out.

William grabbed Benji's chin, turned his face, and kissed him. Hard. All teeth and tongue and intensity. Benji melted toward him, falling over the middle console and banging his elbow on the dash.

William pulled back. "Come on, before I sex you up in the Kum & Go parking lot." He gave Benji one last kiss and got out of the car. Benji followed him in a daze.

They got gas station coffee, which Benji had to admit was better than the stuff he made at home, along with a box of donuts: cinnamon buns with pink frosting, heart-shaped bear claws, and cake donuts with candy hearts on top.

Once they were back in the Alfa, Benji picked a conversation candy heart out of a glob of chocolate icing. "Be My Valentine," he read. "No question mark. Very commanding. I like it." Benji reached over and popped it past William's lips.

William sucked on the candy and smiled. "It's true, isn't it?"

"What is?"

A blush spread across William's cheeks, even pinking up the tip of his nose. "That we're valentines. Real ones."

"Secret valentines," Benji said. "Secret real valentines." He didn't trust that this wouldn't crumble apart at the first sign of trouble, didn't trust that William would want him for longer than a weekend, but he certainly wasn't faking it.

William let loose that adorable smile that absolutely slayed Benji and said, "I can work with that. For now."

When they got back to the lake house, Wren and Robin were doing a stretchy workout on the deck, but they abandoned their efforts for donuts.

William phoned the electric company, and they told him the electricity would be restored by early afternoon, so he informed the remaining guests that the party was back on.

"What do you normally do during this Valentine's Day house party?" Benji asked.

"Watch horror movies, set off fireworks, play beer pong," Wren chirped from her seat on the sofa.

William laughed. "We haven't played a drinking game for years or set off fireworks since that time the cops were called."

Benji had to reevaluate. "You throw ragers." He'd been assuming this was going to be a sedate, mature affair.

"We usually drink, watch movies, play games, and drink some more. We're not wild any longer," William explained.

"I can't imagine you being wild ever," Benji said frankly.

Both Robin and Wren cracked up at that.

"Oh, he has you pegged, Willie," Wren said.

William flushed and fumbled his bear claw, and Benji smothered his laughter into his third donut.

Because they didn't have the ability to watch movies, and no one felt like playing a game, the four of them went on a hike around the lake. By the end of it, Benji had not changed his mind about it being kind of ugly.

Lots of dead grass and mud and a handful of old lake houses, but as the sun glistened through William's dark hair with its silver stripe, Benji could see the appeal. William seemed in his element here—he was wearing *hiking boots*—and a William in his element was a vision to behold. Benji wondered what William was like at a nightclub with strobe lights flashing in his eyes. He probably wore suits and looked magnificent.

When they returned to the house, the power should have been back on. It wasn't.

Benji wasn't worried though. Power companies never got this stuff exact.

By two in the afternoon, William pulled food out of the fridge that he was worried about spoiling. It was a watermelon, a pound of ground beef, a bottle of mayo, and a dozen eggs. For lunch, they'd eaten donuts and Valentine's Day candy.

Robin cut up the watermelon, and they ditched the rest. The ground beef was already room temperature, so they figured it was all a lost cause.

Avi and Manuel arrived at three. Still no power.

Benji had met the men at Sasha's cancelled wedding over three years ago and, like back then, was a bit in awe of the lithe dancers. Avi was serious and broody, Manuel bubbly and effusive.

An hour later, William said, "I should call the power company again, huh?"

Benji was in the kitchen with him, eating salted watermelon straight from the rind. Robin, Wren, Avi, and Manuel were on the dock, drinking and catching up. It was a beautiful day outside, sun shining and a temperature in the mid-forties. Bundled up, it was almost pleasant.

He and William had been stoically not touching all afternoon. It was torture.

"Not a bad idea. If it's not coming back on tonight, we need to prepare." Benji's idea of preparedness would be sharing body warmth with William, but they surely needed to chop wood or something.

Actually, Benji's new idea of preparedness would be watching William chop wood. Ax in hand. Shirtsleeves rolled up his forearms, showing off his dark arm hair. Sweating. Grunting with each swing.

Benji daydreamed as William called, but he could tell it wasn't good news. "What's the verdict?" Benji asked. "Will you have to chop wood to keep us from contracting hypothermia?"

"Huh?" William shook his head, bemused. "They said there was an issue, and it might be five to six more hours."

"That's not so bad. It'll be back on by bedtime. We won't have to cuddle for warmth. We'll just *want* to."

William touched Benji's wrist and flashed him a flirty, private look. "Maybe I should go buy a generator. The closest store that sells stuff like that is probably an hour and a half away. I should have gone yesterday, but I thought we'd have power again by this morning."

"Might not be worth it, then. By the time you're back, the electricity should be nearly back on. Plus, I've kind of enjoyed the adventure."

"Well, I should contact your sister at least," he said. "She and Perry might not want to come."

"Uh, fuck no. She didn't call me when the power went out. You should lie. Tell her everything is A-okay. Here. Give me your phone. I'll do it."

William shoved him away playfully. "Brat." Then William reeled him back in and kissed him.

It was a relief. They both groaned like they'd been denied each other for longer than a few hours. William pushed Benji into the kitchen counter, his hand snaking up the back of Benji's shirt, fingers tripping up his spine.

The front door banged open, his sister's yelled welcome preceding her through the entryway. William jumped back, and Benji flailed, knocking half of the watermelon onto the floor.

Chapter Thirteen

The arrival of Sasha and Perry was a whirlwind of hugs and kisses and congratulations. William hadn't seen them since they'd gotten engaged, and he presented them with a nice bottle of wine as a celebratory present.

Benji cut William with a glare. "Where the fuck did you pull that out of? You said there was no wine last night."

"Well, it was meant to be a present."

William didn't know much about wine, but he'd asked the drink specialist at Sky Bar at the Plaza for a suggestion.

"Take me to your corkscrew, you beautiful man," Perry said, excitement in his voice. Then, "Oh. It's dark in here."

"The power's out."

"Still?" Sasha said. Her short hair was wild from the wind. Or maybe from Perry's hands. Last year, while in that honeymoon phase of a new relationship, they'd been horn dogs around each other, which William happened to think was endearing, luckily.

"I was about to call you," William said. "It'll be out for a few more hours, but should be back on tonight."

"We have flashlights in the emergency kit in Perry's SUV," Sasha said.

"Do you have food in the emergency kit?" Benji asked. "I smashed our only sustenance."

William reached out to ruffle Benji's hair, but aborted the motion at the last second, resulting in a weird little air jab. It was awkward.

"We have peanut butter," William said into the silence that followed.

"Perry's sister sent us with baked goods," Sasha said, and William's mouth automatically watered. "And we brought salad, smoked salmon, crackers, cheese, and summer sausage."

Eventually, Sasha and Perry went back to their car to get the rest of their stuff and William and Benji moved into the kitchen to clean up their watermelon mess.

"You good?" Benji asked.

"Of course. Why wouldn't I be?"

"You're acting strange."

William supposed he was. He wasn't the best at lying, and not showing his attraction to Benji suddenly felt like just that.

It had only been a day.

One day.

Within an hour, everyone sat together in his living

room, the fire roaring, fancy wine in hand, plates of food in their laps. William was thankful for the salad. He needed vegetables. He had a sugar high from Benji and too many heart-shaped bear claws. He hadn't had so many sweets in ages, but Benji had spent most of the afternoon sneaking chocolate candies into William's mouth when no one was watching, and William hadn't been able to turn down that delicious press of fingers on his lips. Not in a million years.

"What should we do first?" Sasha asked, as William quietly melted down because of his secret valentine. "It will need to be something low tech, obviously, since we don't have power."

Wren was curled into Sasha's side. Robin was on her other. The three of them had been thick as thieves for ages. William was thankful that Wren had pulled him along behind her for most of his life, so he didn't miss out on moments like this. He'd taken it for granted for too long though.

"I brought stuff to make Valentine's Day cards," Perry said.

That was met with flabbergasted silence. Then laughter.

Perry blushed but didn't seem too bothered. He looked like a hot tatted lumberjack but was a total romantic. Last year at Valentine's Day, Perry had brought everyone a different romance novel. The one he'd given William had been a fun read. He'd learned some things.

"I'm in," William blurted, the words escaping without forethought.

Benji grinned and said, "Me too." Sasha stared at her brother suspiciously. He raised his eyebrows innocently. "What? I can craft."

Everyone gathered around the table and kitchen counter, candles and lanterns lighting the way. Perry hauled out a big tub of supplies: colorful cardstock, glue, glitter, markers, stencils. It was like a kindergarten classroom in there.

Speaking of kindergarten classrooms. "Sasha, how's Rosie doing? School going well?" William asked, after everyone had been working in companionable silence for a while. He folded his purple cardstock in half.

"She changed schools back in August because he-who-shall-not-be-named eloped with the PE teacher at their old school. It was awkward, so the school system moved them all around." Everyone in the room emphatically cursed Rosie's ex. "She has a date tomorrow with a guy who is really into billiards."

William glanced up from his careful paper cutting. "Is that an innuendo?"

Sasha shook her head. "Nope."

"He has a whole pool-themed room," Benji said wryly. "He sent her pictures. Green felt, far as the eye can see. She was determined to have a date for Valentine's Day even if he sounds hopelessly bland."

Benji was attempting to glue chalky heart candies he'd procured from somewhere into a card, like macaroni art, sans macaroni.

Avi, whose card was black but full of glitter, turned

the music up on his phone and Manuel whooped, distracting everyone. "This is my jam, baby."

"I know," Avi deadpanned. "Anything for you."

Manuel stood up and swept Avi into his arms, leading him into a sexy sway that seemed effortless but was surely practiced. They were a striking couple full of contrasts. Manuel was wearing green chinos and a colorful Hawaiian shirt that popped against his light brown skin. Avi was wearing gray from head to toe.

Wren threw her card on the table. It was orange and pink and intricate. "Teach me, teach me, teach me."

Avi groaned. "You never listen when I try, babe."

"I'll listen," Wren said. "I promise. Willie, get your ass over here. Be my partner."

"Uh, I'd rather not."

She scoffed, skipped over to him, and put her mouth to his ear to whisper, "If you dance with me, I won't spill about that time you got drunk in college and accidentally sent a love letter to your professor. How did you start that email again? 'My Dearest Dr. Glenski. Please can I have an extra week on my term paper? I am enamored by your—'"

He stood up like a puppet master was pulling his strings. Which, he supposed, one was. He glared at her. She'd been holding that dumb email over his head for fifteen years. It had been out of character for him, even then.

"Okay, William. You'll have to take the stick out of your ass for this," Avi said, his voice very matter-of-fact.

With the exception of Wren, William had been

friends with Avi the longest. They'd been college room-mates. He was used to Avi's dryness and the bite in his tone. Underneath it was love.

"I'm standing here, aren't I?"

Avi flashed William a rare smile. "Watch us."

Avi and Manuel demonstrated the move. William had no idea what type of dance this was, but they made it look like sex. They had so much chemistry.

William and Wren tried to copy them. Avi corrected them again and again, until they had it. Or, at least, until they weren't banging their knees together. William glanced up to see everyone staring at them.

"Voyeurs," he called.

"Come on, Benji. Make a woman of me," Robin said, grabbing Benji's hand and pulling him into the living room.

He followed her gamely, hiking his sagging sweats back up his hips. Perry moved behind Sasha, wrapping his arms around her, and they swayed together as they watched.

It was sweet, this moment. Romantic, almost, though William wasn't dancing with the person he wanted to be. Certainly more romantic than any other activities they'd done at this house party in the past.

Eventually, after about a million failed attempts and one "that's adequate" from Avi, William asked, "What dance is this?"

Avi's eyes flared dangerously, which had kind of been William's goal. He liked riling Avi up.

"A rumba," Avi said through gritted teeth.

"It's cute."

"Oh dear. Here we go," Manuel said. He grabbed Avi's shoulders as the man launched into a rant about passion and technique and sensuality.

William glanced at Benji. He was trying to accompany Robin through the sway step, his eyes glued to his feet and his forehead wrinkled in concentration. William's heart launched to the rafters, right out of his chest, like a balloon on a string.

"We'll show them exactly how cute it is. Come on, Manny," Avi snarled. "Back up, everyone. Shoo."

Wren and William laughed as they moved out of the way of the professionals. Sasha restarted the music for them. Then magic happened. Avi smiled so gently at his husband that William's breath caught before Manuel guided Avi through what was frankly the sexiest routine William had ever seen them dance. And he'd seen Avi dance a lot. Partway through the song, Manuel changed something. William couldn't pinpoint it, but suddenly their moves weren't precise and practiced, and they were just dancing with each other, totally in their own world, totally in love. Avi seemed to trust Manuel implicitly to be there at the end of every movement.

William had never trusted anyone like that, and, to be honest, he'd never been able to be reliable in return. He'd never been willing to sacrifice precious time to love, but now he'd opened three clubs, including his baby—Mount. He could finally slow down a bit if he wanted.

William's neck prickled. He met Benji's eyes across the living room. They were full of heat. The song changed to a different beat, and it was an all-out dance party in William's living room. He bowed out, making his way back to the kitchen counter and picking up the Valentine's Day card he'd made. He needed to hide it.

He flipped it open, and the unicorn he'd created glimmered back.

Chapter Fourteen

B enji hadn't been sure what to expect when he'd agreed to come this weekend, but it wasn't a dance party. The sun had set, filling the room with shadows and cozy darkness. The music from Manuel's phone was tinny with lots of reverb but also perfect.

Sweat dripped between Benji's shoulder blades as he shimmied down with Manuel and Avi, a sandwich between them. Manuel had a hand on Benji's abs, and Avi kept laughing huskily in his ear.

Benji closed his eyes and let the adrenaline and dopamine haze rush through him. This was way better than being groped and drunk and full of insecurity at Splat with his friends. He wanted Avi and Manuel to teach him to move his hips independent of the rest of his body, and he wanted to laugh and laugh until he couldn't breathe.

Avi kissed Manuel over Benji's shoulder before playfully shoving Benji out of the way. He landed in Wren's path. Wren, Sasha, and Robin were giggling and vogueing.

William and Perry were sitting on the couch, seemingly enjoying the show. Perry kept laughing at Sasha's antics, totally distracted by her, as always. Benji shucked his sweater off and threw it at William's face. William caught it (with his face) and held it to his nose. Lust shot through Benji's veins. He could feel William's eyes on him, as viscerally as the sweat on his body.

Benji wanted them to dance together. To be sweat and rhythm and the deep bounding bass together. He was nothing if not reckless and great at bad decisions. He took a step toward William. William's eyes went molten behind his tortoise-shell glasses, and he sat up slightly from his relaxed sprawl.

Sasha threw her arm over Benji's shoulders, stopping his forward movement. He snapped his gaze away from William and tried to shake the thirst from his brain.

"I have a present for you."

"Damn right you do," Benji said.

She pulled him over to a tumble of her stuff in the entryway and handed him a brown paper bag. He opened it up and drew out a red silk robe.

"Sasha, it's beautiful."

"There's more in there."

He peeked at the bottom of the bag and grinned. "You're the fucking best."

She smacked a kiss on his cheek, then she hauled him back into the living room and raised her hands. "Bonfire, bonfire!"

He grinned at his sister and joined her chant. "Bon-fire, bonfire!"

William stood up. "We might as well. Not much else to do without power."

"We brought the stuff for s'mores," Manuel chimed in.

"S'mores, s'mores!" Sasha chanted. "Oh, and I have something special to drink too."

Sasha magicked up a bottle of champagne from their cooler. She said they had to drink it now because they couldn't keep it cool in the dead refrigerator.

Logic was nice.

In the end, it was impossible to resist her enthusiasm. He loved that about Sasha. She did everything with her full gut.

William and Avi built the fire on the shore of the lake. William didn't have to chop wood. Benji asked. He had evidently bought a bunch from the Kum & Go before everyone had arrived. Which was a huge shame.

Benji bundled up in every layer of clothing he'd brought and clutched a cold mug of champagne between his hands. They sat in lawn chairs around the fire. He managed to place his next to William's without drawing any suspicion.

Benji was eager to make a s'more, even though William informed him the best time to roast marshmal-lows was after the fire had died to embers. Benji had roasted marshmallows maybe twice in his lifetime. He wasn't willing to wait.

The marshmallows were pink and heart-shaped. Benji

would normally joke about how silly that was. The Valentine's Day markup was probably ridiculous, but as he bit into the s'more, he decided that these babies were no laughing matter.

Benji moaned around the perfect, gooey treat, and William made a choking noise in the back of his throat. Benji licked pink stickiness off his thumb with a smile.

"We should talk about love," Wren said dreamily after a while.

"What about it?" Robin asked. They were sharing a chair and a drink.

"Oh, I know. Best dates," Wren said. "You go first, Robin."

Robin hummed. "I haven't been on a date in ages. Let's see. Once a woman took me to a movie makeup class. We got our faces done up like zombies, then went to a haunted house. I enjoy spooky shit. What about you, Perry? Best date?"

Benji rolled his eyes. Everyone knew what Perry was going to say.

"Once Sasha stood up on stage at a Christmas party and told the whole room she'd made a mistake when she rejected me. Then we danced in the snow and fucked in her VW Bug." Benji snapped his gaze over to them. Perry grimaced. "Oh, oops. Sorry, Benji. TMI."

"Me next!" Manuel said. He was snuggled up on Avi's lap. Avi hid his face in the back of Manuel's neck. "I was on a date with this guy named … uh, what was his name, Avi?"

"Dick."

"Richard. His name was Richard. He was kind of an 'I'm your Daddy, you're my boy' type, which isn't my jam. Anyway, Richard took me to a club. Avi saw me across the bar dancing circles around the guy and asked me if I wanted to dance with someone who could keep up."

"You said yes, and Richard punched me," Avi said, his voice bone dry.

Manuel laughed. "Best date ever. What's your best, love?" he asked his husband.

Avi dug his chin into Manuel's shoulder and said, "Same one," which was about the sweetest fucking thing Benji had ever heard.

William turned toward Benji. "What's your best date?"

"Umm. I don't know."

"Come on!" Wren said. "You're young. Regale us old folks with some stories."

Benji pretended to think for a few seconds.

"Well, I slept with this dude once. It wasn't a date, exactly, but the next morning, we watched the sunrise. He held my hand, and we could see our breath in the air. It was pretty perfect."

Benji couldn't meet William's eyes, but he imagined William being asked his favorite date and saying, "Same one."

"I'll go," Wren said. "In high school, the homecoming king asked me to prom. He ended up making out with his second cousin at the end of the night. It was hilarious."

Everyone gaped. William said, "I told you those Clark boys were no good, Wren."

"Yeah, yeah."

"That's your *best date*?" Benji asked.

She grinned, the fire glinting in her eyes. "He turned out to be a dick. He never lived the whole cousin thing down. Pretty sure they still talk about it at home, don't they, William?"

He shrugged. "Haven't been back in years."

Benji glanced at him, pieces of William's childhood shifting into focus.

"Yeah, you're not great at showing up," Sasha said. "Why would visiting your parents be any different?" Her tone was so offhand it sounded like a joke, but then the air around them sucked down to nothing.

William's heart flopped to his stomach.

"Sasha," Benji said, clearly surprised by her words. She seemed shocked by them too.

William wasn't shocked, really. Just ashamed. What she'd said was true.

Sasha's eyes were wide. "I'm sorry. I didn't mean to say that."

"No, don't apologize," William said. "You're right."

The silence around the circle was earsplitting. Everyone's focus shifted to the crackling bonfire.

"Umm, I'm guessing this is how everyone feels?" William asked, voice shaky.

"You've missed some important things. That's all,"

Wren said, placating like always, first to come to his aid, even when he didn't deserve it.

Sasha sat up in her lawn chair. "I am sorry, William. I shouldn't have said it like that. I know you're busy with your job and stuff comes up, and it's been rough for you while you've built your business."

"But you missed Sasha's wedding. Or, well, the wedding where she was left at the altar," Robin chimed in. William flushed. "And the party after Avi and Manuel opened their studio. And Wren's last runway."

"Shit. Is this an intervention?" Benji asked. "Y'all should have prepared me! I'd have read some info-graphics."

The tension in the circle broke as everyone chuckled. William sent Benji a thankful glance.

"I … uh. I don't have an excuse for being so absent other than the fact that building the business was exhaust-ing," William said finally. "I love you all, and I'm sorry." He took a deep breath. This was painful. "Back in November, I woke up one morning and realized that I hadn't talked to anyone in three weeks who didn't want something from me. I realized that I had money and secu-rity and could actually slow down for once. I realized that I was horrendously unhappy and lonely, and it was my fault. I've not been a good friend, and I hope you can forgive me. I understand if you can't."

The fire snapped, a log rolling and sending up sparks. William, unforgivably, felt as if he might cry. Wren and Sasha both seemed to launch themselves at him, wrap-ping him in a big hug. Maybe he hadn't ruined everything after all. He buried his head in Wren's neck and said, "Thank you. I'm sorry."

"Is that why you've started calling me once a week?" Avi asked, and William laughed a little humorlessly.

"Yeah."

"Do you have 'Call Avi' written in your calendar?"

William rolled his eyes. Avi obviously knew that he did. "I've missed you." He peered around the circle. "I've missed all of you."

"Well, stop. I hate talking on the phone," Avi said, his voice brusque. "If you wanna talk, you need to text me. Or like, drive across town and buy me a drink."

"Deal. Speaking of drinks, I need a refill. Anyone want one?" William really just needed a second alone. Everyone shook their heads. He extricated himself from Wren and Sasha's arms.

Sasha grabbed his hand before he was out of reach. "William," she said softly. "I was being catty, and I apologize for putting you on the spot. I mean it. We're good. We're all good." She gestured at their friends around the bonfire. "I promise."

He lifted her hand to his mouth and kissed her fingers. "It wasn't catty. It was true. And thank you."

He escaped to the house. He needed something stronger than champagne after that.

"You okay?"

The voice behind William made his throat ache. He turned to see Benji, looking serious for once, in the doorway.

William nodded and Benji swooped in for a hug.

"That was kinda brutal," Benji said, whispering in William's ear. "The lonely thing—that's why you've started dating again?"

William nodded again and tucked his face into Benji's neck. "Should have focused on my friends instead."

Benji kissed his ear. "Sounds like you've been trying to do both."

William shrugged.

"You can't change the past, but you're making a change for the future. And you've been nothing but open with me," Benji continued. "You've given me room to be open with you, which has never been easy for me. You're a great guy, William. Everyone out there loves you. They understand."

"And the guy in here with me?"

"Plans to spoil you tonight instead of the other way around."

Chapter Fifteen

B enji waited for William in the master suite again. The electricity had never come on, so Benji was armed with two candles—the rest had been passed out to the others—a spare blanket, and extra wood. Benji, Perry, and Manuel had gone to bed early to let the original friend group patch their shit up.

He could hear laughter downstairs—his sister's brash cackle mingling with Robin's husky chuckle, Wren's giggle, Avi's dry voice, and William's snort—so hopefully, it was all good in the neighborhood.

Benji wanted to blow William's mind, but some gut instinct told him it didn't need to be rockets and acrobatics, that William might need a lighter touch tonight. Benji desperately wanted to be what William *needed*, and that was different than being what the men in his past had *wanted*. Need versus want. It was the difference between kindness and niceness, between acting from the heart or reacting through his insecurity.

These thoughts were spinning through his head as William snuck into his room at one in the morning, a bottle of bubble bath, two glasses, and a bottle of champagne in his arms.

"It's after midnight, so Happy Valentine's Day," William said, his voice a little timid. "You still want me?"

Benji was doomed. He'd been doomed from the start. This beautiful fucker, coming in here all shy and self-conscious and bearing gifts. Want and need, man. Benji needed him, and he'd never, not in a gazillion years, reject William O'Dare, standing there with his heart in his hand.

William had changed out of his jeans and J. Crew sweater and into the pajamas that absolutely turned Benji's crank. He could not handle William in those flannel bottoms.

"Of course. You still want me?"

"More than anything."

"I'd like to do something for you," Benji whispered as he approached William slowly. He took the stuff out of William's arms and deposited it on the floor. "Sit on the bed."

William sat.

"No, wait. Stand up. Take your pants off first." Benji laughed. "Take all your clothes off."

"You too," William said. He threw his bottoms and underwear across the room.

Benji wiggled out of his baggy sweats and his T-shirt. He was wearing a pair of short silk boxers, pink with small red hearts. William touched the fabric at the hem before gazing up at Benji with a lost expression in his eyes. They sat down together on the side of the bed, Benji facing William.

"I'm gonna leave these on," Benji said, gesturing at his boxers.

"Okay."

"This is just for you."

William closed his eyes on a breath. "Okay."

Benji picked up the masturbation sleeve he'd stashed on the bedside table.

"Sasha gave me this today, and I want to use it on you. It's brand new, and I already washed it."

William didn't open his eyes. "What is it?"

"Sasha calls it the Clam Bam, but the official name is the Fleshstroker 2.0. You can pop it open down the long edge, which makes it easier to clean."

"Like a clam."

"Yeah." Benji squirted a bit of lube into the opening of the toy before holding it right at William's tip. "You good?"

"I'm good." William opened his eyes but he didn't look down at the toy as Benji pressed it gently onto his shaft. Instead, he stared at Benji's face, holding eye contact, his eyelashes fluttering a little as the toy bottomed out.

Benji worked him over slowly, watching every flicker of pleasure cross William's face in aching detail. William gripped Benji's thigh, rubbing the silk of Benji's boxers with his fingertips.

"You're hot like this," Benji said. "At my mercy."

"Oh God. You're gonna ruin me, honey."

A shiver travelled up Benji's spine. "Have you ever used one of these?"

William shook his head.

"Do you like it?" Benji moved his hand faster, the lube inside squelching.

"I like you doing it to me. Feels nice to have you so close."

For some reason, that sent a tendril of anxiety through Benji. Those two sentences hadn't been about sex, but intimacy and closeness. Benji didn't know what to do about it.

"So, Mr. Underarms. I could clamp this thing in my armpit and you could fuck it," Benji said brightly, as if he'd just had a brilliant idea. Overcompensation for the win.

William turned his head toward Benji, a laugh tipping his perfect, pink lips. "What in the world?"

"Yeah. Let's do it. It'll be fun." Benji pulled the Flesh-stroker off William's dick, which caused him to let out a moan of loss. Benji loved when he moaned.

"No, wait. I don't want to bagpipe you, Benji."

"Oh. My. God. That's what that's called?"

William laughed helplessly. "I don't want to fuck your armpit. I really don't. But thank you. That is probably the sweetest offer I've ever gotten. Can you keep sitting close to me and doing this? I like this a lot."

Benji smiled. There was humor and light back in William's face, so his suggestion had totally been worth it. Hey, he'd even been willing to give it a shot, but that wasn't what William needed. William needed this—Benji's lips on his ear, shared body heat, gentle hands.

Need versus want.

"I guess we can skip that. *This time*," Benji said, leaning in to mouth at William's neck. "But I'm Googling that next time my phone's not dead. One day, we're gonna get freaky."

William's breath caught on a sharp gasp, but before Benji could suss out that reaction, he twisted the Flesh-stroker back over William's cap, watching it engulf William's frankly gorgeous cock. As Benji slid the toy up, it left a shiny trail of slick behind. A wave of heat wafted off William, and Benji felt taken over by it. His own cock wept out a drop of pre-come, darkening the silk of the boxers.

Within a minute, William's breath was ragged and a sheen of sweat coated his chest. His hips twisted, and he dragged Benji closer, threading his fingers up into Benji's hair.

"Kiss me," William demanded, voice wrecked. "While I come."

So Benji did. He kissed this beautiful mess of a man as he shivered and sighed and died a little under Benji's hands.

———

William placed their two remaining candles around the tub. Since they'd been forced to share most of the candles with everyone else earlier in the evening, it wasn't quite as romantic as the night before, but William was pretty happy with the effect. Benji deserved all the romance, especially after that hand job. William felt incredibly tender toward his valentine just now.

He filled the bathtub with steaming water and two capfuls of the hypoallergenic bubble bath Wren had drunkenly pushed on him before bed because "your skin is sensitive and Happy Valentine's Day and you need to slow down and smell the roses every once in a while, Willie."

When he turned around, Benji was taking a big gulp of champagne. William gently took the glass out of his hand and put it on the lip of the big tub next to the candle. He placed his hands on Benji's hips, tickling the skin above his waistband.

"Can I take these off you?" he asked.

The boxers weren't as showy as some of the things William had already seen Benji in, either in person or in those pics on Benji's phone, but he looked adorably cozy in them.

Benji nodded, his movements loose and languid. Once he was naked, they climbed in together. Benji wiggled back against William's chest, and William brushed his palms over the plains of Benji's body.

"What happened back in November?" Benji asked after a few minutes of uninterrupted touching. "You mentioned that being the impetus for your change?"

William's stomach flopped. "Yeah, but I'm worried it might make me sound selfish and silly."

Benji waved his hand like that didn't matter, flinging water onto the floor. "I won't judge you. Promise."

"Something good happened to me at work."

"What was it?" Benji patted the top of the bubbles with his palms.

"Mount was nominated for best new nightclub. It's the first time a queer space has been a finalist."

"That's great."

"Yeah." William sighed and brushed a puff of bubbles off Benji's ear. "I sent a group text about it. No one really responded. Wren called me a few days later to congratulate me, but it was silence, otherwise. At first I was kind of hurt, but then I realized that it was my fault. You heard all the important life things I've missed out on. Why should they show up for me when I haven't for them? I'd ruined my friendships, like I'd ruined my attempts at relationships."

"You're being too hard on yourself."

"Do you know why I didn't make it to Sasha's disaster wedding three years ago?"

Benji shook his head. "You didn't miss much."

"Yes, I did. I missed being there for someone I love when she was left at the altar. I wasn't there because I accidentally double booked a dinner with big investors. A bunch of things had gone wrong and this was my last chance to secure money from them."

"Did you get the money?"

William's throat squeezed painfully. "Yeah, but I lost something more important, and there are always other investors. I see that now. So I reevaluated my life a bit.

Rearranged some responsibilities with staff and my business partner."

"Decided to find love."

"Yeah. I want what Sasha has. What Avi has. I want a partner to celebrate the good things with. I want to celebrate their good things too."

"Have you ever been in love?" Benji asked.

William kissed Benji's ear. He was getting obsessed with Benji's ears. "The closest I've ever been was with Wren."

He let that sit for a second, worried Benji wouldn't take it well. Instead, Benji laughed. "I should have seen that coming. What happened?"

"I've known Wren since I was thirteen and she was eleven. Grew up together. Wrong sides of the track. I love her more than I've ever loved anyone, but I was self-absorbed. I was too focused on ladder climbing and corporate takeovers and investments to fall in love. And she didn't love me either. We joke that we're soul mates, but we're not *in love*. Never have been, despite trying."

Benji let those words sit between them for a few seconds. Then he said, "I've never had love in the romantic sense or even like what you have with Wren. I love my sisters. They love me, but that's different."

"You're young. There's plenty of time."

William knew immediately that that was the wrong thing to say. Benji didn't tense or freeze up, but the atmosphere around them changed, like he'd checked out emotionally. William wondered if it was the defense mechanism Benji had used in the past with the jerks who wanted him to be different than the brilliant, vibrant man he really was.

William hated that he'd impelled such a reaction. He pressed a kiss to the hinge of Benji's jaw, feeling sandpaper stubble on his lips. "I'm sorry."

"How do you know when love appears, do you think?" Benji touched William's kneecap under the water, tracing it with a fingertip. "I imagine billboards and balloons and hearts in my eyes, but maybe I'm wrong."

The question felt loaded. This whole conversation felt loaded, but William didn't understand why, exactly.

"I think it's quieter than that. It's in the moments of little disaster. The moments when things go wrong, but they're still *so right* because of who you're with. The dropped mugs of coffee and the clothes accidentally ruined in the wash and the …" *The power outages.*

"Grand gestures are nice though," Benji said. "Big public displays of love. Real shouty stuff. Someone proclaiming, 'I love *this* person, in all their glory, *so there.*'"

"So there," William echoed. He hoped Benji got that one day. Benji deserved it. He deserved the big "shouty" proclamation. To be shown that he was loved with no reservations or stipulations.

"Yeah." Benji looked over his shoulder, giving William a huge grin.

William stroked the side of Benji's face, inadvertently soaking it with bubbles. They both laughed. William took his mouth in a searing, soap-scented kiss.

They made out lazily in the darkness, no big rush to reach a destination, just enjoying the ride. William wanted so many things, even though his body was sated and tired and done for the night. He wanted to ask Benji to stand so William could eat his glorious ass. He wanted to kiss Benji's chin. He wanted to see Benji's eyelashes clumped and wet in the humid air. He wanted to turn Benji around, watch the puffs of soap caress and slide off his shoulders as Benji came on his face. He wanted to taste that lush divot in Benji's bottom lip.

But this was good too. William put his mouth to the warm shell of Benji's ear and whispered praise and curse words and pleas. Benji lifted a long, gorgeous leg out of the water and planted his foot on the lip of the tub, opening himself up to William's hands. So William touched him, mapped the length of his thigh and the tendon of his groin. Yes, this was good.

It was good as William tripped a finger up Benji's cock. As William's fingertips trailed over Benji's hole, skin soft from the water.

It was good, so good, as Benji's breath hitched in his throat, and he flung his head back against William's chest.

Light.

Light so bright that William thought it was in his head, his mind a rampage of rawness and happiness and desire.

But Benji jumped and hissed, "*Fuck.*" He stood, water and bubbles sluicing off his glorious body and falling over William. "Fuck fuck fuck. William, get up."

"Huh?" William closed his eyes against the pain in his retinas. "Shit."

"Yeah. *Shit.* Come on. Every light in the house just turned on."

William's body mourned the loss of Benji in his arms, and his mind couldn't catch up. He sat and scrubbed a hand over his face. Benji was already drying off with a towel, his movements jerky and frantic.

"Holy smokes, get a move on!" Benji tossed a towel at William's head. William caught it and stared at him. "William," Benji said, his voice a low whine. "They're going to discover you're not in the sunroom if you don't hurry your ass up."

Oh. Right.

They were a secret.

William didn't exactly want to explain the secret valentines thing his best friends in the middle of the night, but Benji's apparent fear of it hurt.

William dried off in record time, threw his clothes back on, and reached the landing of the second floor as Perry opened his and Sasha's door and stepped out.

Perry was rubbing sleep out of his eyes as he said, "Hi." He didn't seem confused by William's presence on a floor he had no reason to be on tonight.

"Uh, hey. Hi."

Benji tiptoed down the stairs behind him, pulling William's attention like a magnet. Both of them had wet hair. Jesus Christ, they were obvious.

"Need help turning out the lights and plugging appliances back in?" Perry asked.

William nodded. "Yeah. Thanks."

Perry led the way down the stairs, followed by Benji

and William. When they reached the ground floor, William could see Wren standing at the entrance to the sunroom, probably wondering where the hell he was. He tensed.

She turned as she heard them. William knew her pretty well, but he couldn't read her expression at all in that moment. Maybe delight. Maybe suspicion.

The four of them systematically took care of the lights and appliances downstairs. Wren was sleepy-drunk, and she gave William a hug before heading back to bed. Benji pretended to be distracted by a chocolate cupcake.

Perry clapped a hand on Benji's shoulder. "You okay? Gonna head back up?"

Benji nodded and shoved some cupcake into his mouth. Around his bite, he said, "In a 'econd."

Once Perry went upstairs, Benji turned toward William, his mouth still full of chocolate. William grinned and snatched Benji to him, nipping playfully along his neck. Benji tasted slightly astringent from bubble bath not fully rinsed off, but the underlying sweetness of his skin soon met William's tongue.

Benji groaned and went pliant against him, but he didn't stop eating the cupcake.

"We should go to bed," William said, kissing the words into Benji's throat.

"Mmmhmm." Benji pulled back, biting his lip on a smile. "Maybe your house is full of prudish little fairies, always cock-blocking us."

"It just might be."

"Maybe tomorrow we should fuck in the sunroom. It's

easier for me to lie about why I'm downstairs than for you to explain why you're on the third floor."

"Sure." William wanted to pull Benji into the sunroom now, but this was nice too, especially as Benji's eyes went hooded and his mouth went soft. Benji thumbed William's bottom lip, and it took William a second to realize Benji had spackled chocolate icing on it.

Benji followed his thumb with a lazy, lush kiss. A kiss that could make a man lose his head. It tasted of chocolate and champagne.

A word burst from William's lips fully formed and urgent. "*Sweetheart.*"

Benji made a gutted noise in his throat, and that sound wrenched something in William's heart. Then Benji was hugging him, gripping him tight and undoubtedly smearing cupcake down his back.

"Happy Valentine's Day," Benji whispered.

And William couldn't let him go, so he didn't. He dragged Benji into the sunroom, laid him down, and held him until morning.

Chapter Sixteen

With morning, and electricity, came responsibilities, but William wanted this—Benji spooned in front of him, their body weight making the middle of the air mattress sink, the scent of watermelon in his nose—for a few minutes longer.

Borrowed time. William normally thought of that phrase in regards to his work, but this morning it applied. At any moment, the rest of the house would awaken, and William would have to check his email, and this fuzzy, wonderful bubble he and Benji had been living in would burst.

Benji stirred against him, his legs rustling the blankets. "Morning." Benji's voice was rough from sleep. When all was said and done, they'd only gotten a few hours.

"Morning, beautiful."

Benji let out a happy, little hum. "Can we watch the sunrise from here?"

"Of course."

That was what they did, despite the fact that it substantially increased the likelihood they'd get caught.

As the thin, blueish light transformed into faint pinks and peachy oranges and golden yellows, Benji turned over and kissed William's cheek.

"I don't know what this is between us. It kind of started as a joke, or an excuse, maybe. Like I wanted to sleep with you, so boom, we'll be valentines and that gives me a legit reason to put my hands in your pants. It doesn't feel like a joke or an excuse anymore, William."

"Go on a date with me."

"What?" Benji blinked a few times, his eyes stormy blue. "Really?"

"Yes. I'm sorry I let you think that this was simply practice for me as I get back out in the dating world, but it's more than that now. I don't want to *practice* with you. I want to go on a date with you."

"What if it's a horrible date? I could add to your bad-date batting average."

"Then we decide if we want to go on another one, you goober."

Benji smiled shyly, and William was once again amazed by this man who could be shy about going on a date but posted pictures of himself in lingerie and wore neon-orange ponchos and danced with no reservation.

"I'll think about it," Benji said. Before William's brain could catch up to the pseudo-rejection, Benji changed the subject. "What's the plan for today?"

William's own barriers started coming back up, creaking into place. "I need to get some work done."

"Ah. Okay." Benji pressed a short kiss to William's lips. "I'll let you get to it."

Benji rolled off the air mattress and was out of William's hands before William could grab him back.

"I didn't mean right this instant."

Benji shot him a wide grin. It felt fake. "I need to pee. And need coffee. You better have coffee."

Then he was gone, slipping through the door to the sunroom and leaving William barely treading water in his wake.

The rest of the morning dripped slowly by as everyone took turns showering. Perry got the craft box back out, and Benji seemed totally immersed in it. He was wearing the red silk robe Sasha had gotten him over a T-shirt and workout leggings. The robe kept slipping off his shoulder as he glued those candy hearts inside a card. William wanted to get a closer look but wasn't brave enough.

Sasha sidled up to William as he ate a cupcake for breakfast. She knocked their shoulders together and poured him a mimosa.

"I love you. You know that, don't you?" she said.

"I do. I love you too."

Last night, after Benji had "gone to bed," William had hashed everything out with Sasha, Avi, Robin, and Wren. He realized he wasn't the only one who'd been all up in his feelings. Avi and Manuel were thinking of adopting a baby. Robin was stressed about expanding into the lube market. Sasha had recently had a breakdown about her impending nuptials. And Wren, well, she was clearly enamored with a married couple and didn't know what that meant for her. They'd all agreed that a house party once a year wasn't an adequate amount of friendship time, not when they lived in the same city.

"I want you to be happy," Sasha said. "Wren and I were talking about your dating dilemma. I have thoughts."

"Of course you do," he grumbled, but inside, he was pleased she wanted to talk to him, period. If only he could say, "I'm falling for your brother. How's that for a dilemma?"

"You need to think outside the box," Sasha said.

"In what way?"

"All the ways. What activities you do for dates, where you find dates, the type of person you go on dates with."

"Sounds simple," he said wryly, and she laughed.

"I think it is. I think you know it is too." With that *mysterious* statement, she left him in the kitchen to sit with her brother. Benji wordlessly handed her some candy hearts, and she popped them into her mouth.

By eleven, Benji was several mimosas in, and didn't seem to care that everyone could see him throwing William bedroom eyes. Hell, William didn't care either. He loved it.

Benji skipped up to him, thrust a glass of grapefruit mimosa—pink for Valentine's Day—into William's hand and said, "Help me pick my next Instagram picture."

"Okay," William said. He glanced over Benji's shoulder. Avi was watching them, a small, sly smile on his face. "What type of vibe are you going for?"

Benji stepped even closer, their hips touching. He stole William's drink to take a sip. When William lifted the cup back to his own mouth, the glass was warm from Benji's lips.

"Hmmm. Dark and vampy, I think," Benji said. "With a bit of an anti-Valentine's Day message."

William's mouth went dry. He wanted Benji to have a good Valentine's Day, to want to celebrate it rather than denigrate it, but William also really wanted to see him in something vampy.

William growled, "You're a tease, you know that?"

"I know that," Benji said, nodding very seriously.

"I like this one with the fishnets all over."

"It's a bodysuit."

"Yeah. That one. It's kind of asstastic though, so if you don't want your full crack on the Internet, I'd go with the—"

"Did you just say asstastic?"

William flushed.

Benji laughed loudly, attracting the eyes of everyone in the living room. He dropped his voice, "Am I rubbing off on you, William?"

"Not currently," William sassed back.

"Maybe later." Benji tapped out a caption. William could see the word "asstastic" in all caps, but other than that, he didn't read it fast enough. He'd have to follow Benji so he didn't miss a post. "Sasha said that we could play poker soon, and that you could teach me."

"Oh, Sasha volunteered me, did she?"

Benji nodded and took another sip of the drink he'd made for William.

"When?" William asked.

"Whenever you can?"

William nodded. "Let me reply to some emails first, then I'll teach you."

"Thank you, thank you, thank you." Benji bopped William on the chest, chin, and nose.

They stared at each other for a loaded moment. William wanted to kiss him, and it was clear that Benji wanted that too. There was a hole where the natural action would have been. Benji shook his head and bounded off. William met Sasha's eyes across the room and flushed, wondering if that gap where the kiss should have been was as obvious to the others as it was to him.

He went to his office. Wren's suitcase had exploded in there, but he hardly noticed. He fell into his desk chair and took a few deep breaths.

It was going to be okay. Benji would or wouldn't take him up on the date. They would or wouldn't work out in the real world. The universe did not end and begin on the lost kiss of a beautiful twenty-four-year-old man.

Emails. William needed to focus on the emails.

It wasn't hard to do. There were a shit ton of them.

A gazillion deleted emails and four phone calls later, Benji stepped into the office.

William jumped. He'd been in his own world. "Hi, sweetheart."

"Hey." Benji closed the door most of the way behind him, but didn't latch it. "I decided to rescue you."

"How long have I been in here?"

"Over an hour."

William closed his eyes. Here he was, making the exact same mistakes he'd always made. "I'm so sorry."

Benji shrugged and moseyed over to the squat bookcase in the corner. It was full of old college textbooks. "It's fine. I don't mind. You lost several days to the power outage. Your job is important, William. Don't feel guilty about being good at it, *but* we're eating lunch, and I will eat your entire helping of pancakes if you don't get your ass out there."

"Where did the pancakes come from?"

Benji froze, hovering halfway over the bookcase.

"Benji? Everything okay?"

Benji stood up abruptly. "Huh?"

"Where did the pancakes come from?" William repeated.

"Manuel went to the store for ingredients." His voice sounded odd. Not bad, exactly, but a little artificial.

"Come here."

With a slight shrug, like he was shaking off a fly, Benji stepped over Wren's cosmetics bag to land on William's lap.

"Hi, valentine," William said, pressing a tiny kiss to his cheek.

Benji blinked a few times, nodding to himself. Then he kissed William, dirty and wet and full of need.

172

Benji was breathless, and not because he was kissing William like there was no tomorrow.

That paper on the bookcase. Fuck.

What had the title been? "Prospective Partner Criteria."

Benji licked into William's mouth. He didn't want to face this yet. Bullet points danced in his mind's eye though.

- *Thirty-five or older*
- *Business professional or business owner with high investment in career*

William cupped Benji's shoulders. It felt spectacular to be held and caressed. Almost spectacular enough to distract him.

- *Must like nonfiction,* The New Yorker, *and true crime podcasts*

What the hell was that? *Must like,* it said. As if people who didn't read nonfiction were somehow not smart enough for William.

Was he too young for William? Not successful enough? Acceptable for a fling but nothing else?

- *Serious demeanor, thoughtful, good taste*

That last one burned Benji's retinas. Serious, thoughtful, tasteful. Benji really wasn't any of those things.

Someone else had written, "Doesn't want a sugar daddy," followed by "Must throw down in the kitchen" at the end of the list. Benji couldn't even do the easiest thing on the list. He was a trash cook.

And the sugar daddy thing … it highlighted their differences. Benji didn't want a sugar daddy. It had never crossed his mind, but he did want William, and there was a disparity there. Benji was solidly blue collar, solidly lower-middle class. William could actually be a sugar daddy if he wanted. That type of financial solvency was unfathomable to Benji.

Shit, shit, shit.

William pulled back, biting Benji's bottom lip before releasing it. "What's wrong?"

"What?" Benji asked.

"You seem distracted. Are you okay?" William's burnt-caramel brown eyes were full of concern.

Benji tapped the edge of William's glasses playfully. "I'm fine."

And he was. He would be.

He'd milk this secret valentines thing for all it was fucking worth. He was going to keep sneaking kisses and sex and fun until their time was up, and time was going to be up soon. He was going home tomorrow. He'd never be William's ideal prospective partner, and he wasn't going to try to be. He was never going to *try* to be someone's perfect partner ever again. One day it would be right, and he would be good enough. Today just wasn't that day.

Chapter Seventeen

B enji spent most of the day with a low-key buzz, which was not a bad state in which to while away one of the worst holidays of the year.

He'd managed to act normal around William, despite not feeling normal at all. He'd finished his Valentine's Day card (those stupid candy hearts would not stay glued) but had no idea if he'd work up the guts to give it to William.

Now, he had his head in Sasha's lap. Perry was on her other side, dozing. William, Robin, Manuel, and Avi were playing poker at the kitchen table. Benji had sucked at poker. Wren was painting tiny black hearts onto her nails by the fire.

Wren was drunk, but it wasn't affecting her nail-art ability. She'd promised Benji she'd do him next. Sasha was also drunk. They were fun drunks—cuddly and giggly and pleasant. Benji tended to get teary-eyed when inebriated (or after he had mind-blowing sex with William, evidently), but his sister was the opposite.

Sasha combed her fingers through Benji's hair. She was brainstorming sex toy ideas for Lady Robin's fantasy line—Monster Me—and he was watching the "likes" tick up on the photo he'd posted on Instagram earlier. He already had thirty, which wasn't that many, but considering he'd started the weekend with zero followers, it was kind of exciting.

"So, baby brother … did my evil plan work?" Sasha asked him out of the blue.

"What evil plan?"

"My evil plan not to tell you that the party had been postponed."

He frowned and glanced up at her, dropping his phone onto his stomach. He'd decided not to be mad at Sasha for being a forgetful flake. Presents made him very forgiving, and she'd brought him a sex toy and a beautiful silk robe. The robe was silky and the color of blood, and he'd already put the sex toy to good use.

"That was on purpose?" he asked.

She nodded. "Sure was, bub."

"Why in the world would you do that?" He sat up. Wren turned to watch them while blowing on her fingernails. He narrowed his eyes. "What's going on?"

Sasha sighed. "I'm drunk. Don't listen to me. Do you think people would fuck a White Walker dildo? I'm pretty positive *I* would, but that might be the wine."

"Don't change the subject, Sasha Holiday! And yes."

Wren nodded very seriously, but Benji didn't know if

it was in response to Sasha trying to wiggle her way out of a confrontation or the White Walker thing.

"What are you talking about?" Perry asked, waking up at the worst possible moment.

"Nothing," Sasha said smoothly.

This thing between him and William had been a setup? Was William in on it?

No. William had been too shocked and awkward on Thursday when Benji had arrived.

Dread bloomed in Benji's gut. He didn't want to be manipulated into anything. That was exactly what he'd been running away from. He wanted to be in control of his decisions, especially ones about his bleak-ass love life. He didn't want to fall in love because his nosy sister had pushed a hot, unsuspecting guy in his path.

And he didn't want William to find out this had been orchestrated. That would be one more knock against Benji. Right up there with his blue-collar job and his lack of interest in murder podcasts!

"Sasha," Benji bit out. "What the fuck? Your romance-reading boy toy has scrambled your brain."

"I do prefer boy toy to fiancé. Thank you for remembering that," Perry said.

"You're welcome," Benji said. "Sasha, come with me, please." He pulled Sasha off the couch and into the entryway for some privacy.

"I worry about you, Benji," she said once they were alone.

He rolled his eyes. "You shouldn't. I'm fine. I've got two meddling sisters I love. I have a job I'm great at. A truck that gets me laid. Things are swell." He did love his sisters and his job, but the rest was bullshit.

"You been withdrawn lately, like a cloud descended on you. That's why I—"

"Manipulated me into showing up here early in the hopes William would bang the sad from my eyes?" he asked, cutting her off.

She shrugged. "It was a spur-of-the-moment decision, not a thought-out manipulation. Anyway, I did it as much for him as you. He needs someone as vibrant as you in his life. Someone to show him what he's missing by walling himself off. I wanted you to be friends."

"You are not my madam, Sasha. Don't pimp me out to your lonely friends."

She laughed. "Did it work?"

Benji did something he very rarely attempted with either of his older sisters. He lied through his fucking teeth. "I got him to eat pizza and wear pajamas for a whole day, if that counts."

"It does. Friendship is just as good."

"Yeah. It is."

Robin barreled around the corner, surprising them both. "Everything okay?" she asked.

They both nodded.

Robin was wearing an overexcited grin Benji had never seen on her face. "I have an awesome idea."

"What is it?" Benji asked.

After a few beats of dramatic silence (Robin was amazing at drama—she was Lady Robin after all), she said, "Spin the Bottle."

Benji was, of course, game, and it was no shocker that Robin had suggested it. She was like the orgy queen. Kissing lots of people was kind of her jam, but he was surprised to find that everyone else was game too. These thirty-somethings were fun.

Once it was established that Benji and Sasha wouldn't have to kiss each other, they all settled into a circle in front of the fireplace, thereabouts where he and William had fucked two days ago (oops).

Perry gently placed an empty red-wine bottle in the middle of the circle and Sasha passed out champagne. The fire crackled and cast a warm, ruddy glimmer around the room.

Robin went first since the game had been her idea. The bottle landed on Avi. His smile was slightly predatory as she crawled across the circle toward him, her tawny skin radiant in the firelight. They kissed with no preamble.

They seemed very familiar with each other. And with kissing each other.

Benji's brain exploded. He glanced around the circle. Had everyone here slept with each other? That was kind of wonderful and weird and oddly appealing. Not that he wanted to sleep with anyone here besides William, but he liked that this group was so open with each other.

He suddenly felt young and naïve.

The game continued on with Avi getting to kiss his husband (boring), Manuel kissing Perry (decidedly *not* boring), Perry kissing Wren (super chastely), before Wren's spin landed on William.

Wren said, "For old time's sake?"

Her kiss was short and smacking. Not sexy at all.

"This group is sort of incestuous, isn't it?" Benji said.

"Please don't use the word incestuous in my presence," Sasha sassed. They both laughed.

"For real, though." Benji took a slug of his champagne, realizing that he was perhaps a bit tipsy. "Who here has slept together? Cone of silence, I swear."

Robin shrugged. "I haven't slept with anyone in this room, but I've kissed most of them. I like kissing. Obviously." She gestured grandly to indicate the whole of their party game.

Wren leaned into the middle of the circle to meet Sasha's eyes.

Sasha shrugged. "I don't mind. You?" She looked at Perry. Perry shook his head.

"Okie dokie. I've slept with William, years ago, and Sasha and Perry," Wren said. Benji choked on his drink. He'd always pegged Perry as a bit innocent, but innocent men didn't have threesomes, right?

Manuel and Avi were, apparently, into watching other people but didn't join in.

"And you, William?" Benji asked, trying to smother his grin.

"Well, Wren. And Avi kissed me once when we were twenty."

"That was after you told your accounting professor about your amorous feelings via email while asking for a deadline extension," Avi said, chill as ever. "You'd been moping for a week, so I asked Wren what was up with you. I thought a kiss would heal the sting of embarrassment."

Amusement and noise exploded in the circle at that evident bombshell. William's eyes flashed wide, and he playfully glared at Wren. She was laughing so hard tears were leaking out of her eyes.

Benji was also intensely aware of the love in this house. This oddball group of friends loved each other, and it had nothing to do with sex. They might not see each other very often or talk all the time, but they loved each other.

Benji was fucking jealous.

"Spin the bottle, William," Wren said, her voice teasing.

William spun the bottle and, unfortunately, it landed on Sasha. They pecked quickly, laughter burbling from Sasha's lips. When Sasha spun the bottle, it settled on Benji.

They both groaned. Per their agreed upon rules, Sasha got to kiss her fiancé and also choose who Benji would kiss instead of her. She pretended to hem and haw before saying, "William!"

Benji tried to school his expression by taking a long drink, the bubbles tickling his nose. William was directly across from him, so he slinked across the middle of the circle and into William's space.

Benji kissed him softly, just a small press of lips, but it was as sweet as the champagne bursting on his tongue. He sighed and pulled back, not wanting to clue everyone—especially his matchmaking sister—into his attraction to this man. Secret valentines were secret.

With an ornery pat on William's cheek, Benji said, "Thanks, old man," causing an eruption of laughter around the room.

<hr>

William's heart was hammering in his ears, but he tried to play it cool. "Is it my turn to spin or Benji's?"

"Who cares?" Robin said. Her cheeks were scarlet and she was lounging back on her elbows, clearly happy with how this game was going. "There's no loser. Benji, spin."

Benji twisted the bottle, letting it fly. It landed on Manuel.

"Oh *heyyy*!" Benji said.

Manuel was sitting next to William, so William had a great view as Benji pressed his wide, perfect mouth to Manuel's smiling lips. It was over fast, but when Benji pulled back, he winked at William.

As the minutes ticked on, and the game continued, William ached for the man across from him. It was almost unbearable not to kiss him, not to grab Benji and taste his mouth after Wren fed Benji a chocolate-covered strawberry.

William was certain he was the only one burning alive. All his friends were choking on laughter and enjoying the silliness of the game, but he was on fire. He felt invaded by his desire to savor the lushness of Benji's mouth. To claim him in private and in public and during a game of fucking Spin the Bottle.

Wren twirled the wine bottle, and it landed on Benji. William's heart soared from his chest. Benji would get to spin next. William started doing math in his head. Eight people in the circle, seven people the bottle could land on, one of those people—Sasha—Benji couldn't kiss.

Wren grabbed Benji by the ears and kissed him. William's mouth went dry with anticipation

A one in six chance. A 16.67 percent chance Benji's spin would land on him.

Benji glanced at William through his golden lashes and spun the bottle. It whirled, moving in a blur before slowing and slowing and slowing, tipping achingly past Wren, past Avi, past Manuel before teetering to a stop on William.

William downed the rest of his champagne. Benji crawled toward him slowly, his eyes alight and teasing. That was not going to stand this time.

As soon as Benji was within arm's reach, William hauled him forward, his hands swamping Benji's cheeks and jaw. Benji had to scramble closer on his knees so he didn't lose his balance. Up on his knees, Benji was taller than William, but William was going to control this kiss. He held Benji's head steady and slanted his mouth to get a better angle.

Sasha hooted and said, "Slip him the tongue, Benji."

Benji did. He licked over William's lips with a near silent growl. Then their tongues were sliding together, wet and warm. Benji's hands came down on William's shoulders before skating up to his neck. William threaded one hand into Benji's hair, cupping the back of his head.

Red-hot sparks flashed behind William's eyelids and buzzing filled his ears. He kissed Benji with his whole heart. Kissed him like the world was disintegrating around them.

Slowly, sounds in the room started to filter through William's haze. Laughing and clapping and people throwing stuff at them. William smiled against Benji's mouth. Then, with an irrepressible laugh, William tipped Benji into a pseudo-dip, spinning him off his knees and backwards over William's lap, never stopping the kiss. He quickly righted Benji and pulled back.

Benji swayed. He touched his lips in what appeared to be a bit of a daze.

William ruffled Benji's hair and said, "Thanks, kiddo."

Benji grinned and pretended to swoon back into William's lap. William caught him and kissed him. Again. And harder.

Chapter Eighteen

____

When the kisses ended, Wren leaned across the circle to slap William's shoulder. "Add that to your stupid criteria, William. Damn."

William blushed, feeling suddenly exposed, and Benji scrambled out of his arms with an awkward laugh.

That list of dating criteria was a crock of shit. He had essentially described himself, which wasn't dating criteria so much as an ego stroke.

The game broke up after that. Benji avoided him for the rest of the night, and Avi gave William his condolences on getting shot down by a younger man. Evidently, their secret was still intact.

William hoped their arrangement was as well.

That night, he snuck into Benji's room once the house quieted. William had planned a seduction. He evidently didn't need one because Benji leapt into his arms as soon as he crossed the threshold. Benji had commandeered a handful of candles to light the way and started a fire in the wood-burning stove. It felt like romance to William. He hoped it was romance.

They kissed. Or maybe they devoured. Whatever it was, they ended up pressed against the wall.

Benji let the red silk robe fall into a puddle at his bare feet. He lifted his arms, so William took his shirt off. They didn't speak as they finished undressing. Whatever was happening was too big to talk about. Benji's leggings hit the floor, and William's breath caught.

Velvet and silk. Deep, rich red. William's fingertips trembled over the fabric of their own volition, like his brain hadn't caught up with what he was seeing beyond smooth, warm, indulgent. He had to touch. He couldn't stop wanting to touch. Benji's cock stiffened right before William's eyes.

They were paneled briefs, with silk in the front and sides of velveteen. The velvet was rich under William's fingertips.

"Beautiful."

"Really?" Benji asked.

"God, yes. Of course, really."

A blush darkened Benji's cheeks, and he looked so painfully perfect that William's knees went weak.

"Wish you could take another picture of me in these, but my phone died," Benji said.

"Next time. Next time you wear them, I'll take your picture."

That statement sat between them heavily. Benji had never responded to William's request for a date. William had no idea if there would be a next time. And yes, this statement was wrapped up in sex, but that didn't mean it wasn't real. That didn't mean it wasn't what William wanted.

Benji rested his forehead on William's shoulder, and an unquenchable, unbelievable tenderness hit William in the solar plexus. He wrapped his palms around Benji's hips, his thumbs hooking on God's gift to hipbones, and pushed Benji into a miniscule version of the box step Avi had taught them.

Benji didn't raise his head, but whispered, "I wanted to be dancing with you yesterday."

"Me too."

Stepping in a square was the extent of William's ability, but Benji started humming a love song, so William kept swaying him through it. Finally, Benji lifted his head and gazed directly into William's eyes.

The air was crackling with possibility and a hushed need. It felt like they were both on the brink of saying foolish things.

William opened his mouth. Drew in a breath. Pinched Benji's chin between his thumb and forefinger.

And Benji grabbed William's dick. William's mind reeled away from all the honeyed words he'd been about to unleash.

"Want you," Benji said against William's mouth. "Want you to take me apart. Make me feel good. Make it feel special." There was a tenor of desperation and pain in Benji's voice that William had never heard, and he had no idea what made this time different than the times before.

William tried to slow the jackrabbit pounding of his heart to focus, truly focus, on what his valentine needed. "What's something you love but haven't done in a while?"

William was expecting it to be simple, like reverse cowgirl, but Benji went shy and stuttery, ducking his head and fiddling with the waistband of his briefs. William put his lips to Benji's ear and whispered, "You can tell me. We don't have to do it, whatever is making you blush like that, but you can tell me. We can talk about it."

Benji pressed closer to William, notching his forehead into William's neck. "So I have a toy that I can use to come, uh, basically hands free? But sometimes it doesn't work, or it takes a long time, so it's not great for partners. I get distracted by it. Become self-absorbed."

"There is nothing self-absorbed about that. Do you want to show me? You don't have to."

"What would you do while I'm ... *you know*."

William licked the soft spot under Benji's ear. "Watch you. Maybe touch you, if that was okay. Touch myself."

"It'll be boring for you."

William's heart broke that someone at some point had made Benji believe he was boring or wrong or not enough. He was more than enough. He was everything.

"It won't be. I promise. But if you want to do something else, we absolutely can."

Benji drew in a deep breath and a new determination flashed in his eyes. "No. I want to show you. I like the thought of you watching me. Let me grab the toy."

William followed Benji's lead in a daze as Benji pulled a slightly curved metal rod out of his bag. It was maybe six inches long and one inch in diameter with a tapered bulb on each end. He handed it to William.

"Holy fuck, this is heavy."

"Yeah. It's stainless steel."

Benji slipped his underwear down to his knees, sat with his shoulder blades against the headboard, and planted his feet close to his ass. The shock of dark red velvet against his thighs, preventing him from spreading his legs very far apart, was sexy in a way William didn't really understand.

"You can help with this part," Benji said, already breathless.

"Okay."

"Lube this up and put it in me."

William followed directions, smiling at their role reversal. He'd fall all over himself to be who Benji needed him to be.

Benji's eyelashes fluttered, and he let out a dirty grunt once the bulb slipped in. William gave it an experimental little thrust. "What next?"

Benji took hold of the base of the toy, and William let go, ready to just watch.

Then a brilliant idea hit William. "Could I sit behind you?"

Benji wordlessly scooted forward. William slid behind him, and Benji settled back into the same position between William's legs, but leaning against William, not the headboard. At this angle, Benji's shoulder blades and spine pressed into William's chest.

From his view over Benji's shoulder, William could see

the hills and valleys of Benji's body. He could feel every twitch of Benji's muscles as Benji started to slowly, almost imperceptibly, move the wand.

William relaxed against the headboard and wrapped an arm around Benji, pressing his palm over Benji's heart. The heartbeat was strong and fast, jumping to meet William's hand.

After a few minutes, Benji's breathing suddenly shallowed out, and his legs started to shake.

"You feel so good in my arms," William whispered into the damp hollow of Benji's neck, Benji's sweat a gift on his tongue. Benji let out a needy, stifled cry and clamped his free hand down on the thigh William had braced outside Benji's own.

Benji's movements with the toy became longer. Harder. His heartbeat was lightning quick under William's hand.

William was struck by Benji's vulnerability in that moment. Benji's head was flung back on William's shoulder, totally trusting, his eyes closed, his body quaking. His face was criminally hot.

"Need," Benji mumbled.

"What do you need, baby?"

A gut-punching moan slipped out of Benji's mouth. "I don't know."

"You can get there," William said. He slipped his hand down Benji's stomach and found a dribble of pre-come with his thumb. William lifted his thumb to his own mouth, tasting salt.

"Hold me … steady."

"I will," William said. "I will, Benji. Always."

Benji's body flushed hot, and he would have been embarrassed about the noise he made, but there was no room for embarrassment right now.

William tightened his arm around Benji's chest, and with his other hand, he reached around Benji to grab the velvet underwear binding Benji's knees close together. William didn't do anything other than clutch the taut, stretched-thin briefs in his fist. Didn't try to move Benji or change his angle.

He held him like he wanted Benji to feel grounded and surrounded and safe. And Benji did. This would likely be the last time he had this, *had William*, and Benji wasn't going to take it for granted.

Benji was getting close. It was quicker than normal, and he didn't know if it had to do with William's breath in his ear or the warmth at his back or the fingertips digging into his pec.

He moved the steel toy harder against his prostate, massaging it in rough, quick jabs. A steady trickle of pre-come slicked his cock, and he focused on the heat blooming inside him, on clenching his pelvic floor, on breathing in time with his muscle contractions. He fell headfirst into the blood-red darkness as his vision wavered and his eyes rolled back.

Spunk flowed out of him in a sudden rush. He cried out and twisted in William's arms as his release switched to hard pulses and spurts and radiating heat from the very core of him.

"Oh God, oh God, oh God," Benji chanted as he peaked, then plateaued.

William kissed Benji's neck through the last throbs of his orgasm. When William pulled back, Benji was dazed and hazy. Wet warmth covered his stomach, dripping down his sides onto William's legs. Benji was coated in sweat.

William put his hand in front of Benji's mouth, "Spit, beautiful."

Benji did without thought. Just spit right into William's hand. William was shaking, nearly as much as Benji. He moved the hand behind Benji's back to grip his own dick.

"No. Fuck me, please," Benji said.

William let out a trembling breath. "You sure?"

"Yeah." Benji might not be able to come again, but he wanted the intimacy of holding William within his body. He felt so close to William already.

He wanted to be closer.

William tumbled Benji onto his back, and within the space of a handful of breaths, the dildo was gone, a condom was on, a mess of lube was slicked over both of them, and William was at the precipice of Benji's body.

"Are you sure?" William asked again.

"I am."

William still had a hold of Benji's favorite briefs (he had three velvet pairs but *these* were his favorite), using the fabric to push Benji's knees toward his chest. The way

William used that slip of underwear was control and command and power.

The first thrust inside whited out Benji's brain. He'd been here before—underneath a man, his body an impetus for pleasure—but it had never been like this. The lingering worries in the back of his mind, worries of stupid criteria and William's feelings and the future, floated away.

William was *watching* him, mapping Benji with his eyes, seeing elemental desires Benji had never let other people see. William gave voice to them softly, sweetly.

Words like, "Let me in," which Benji followed with, "Take it."

Words like, "Beautiful," and "Strong," and "Brave," which Benji followed with, "Harder."

Cries and shivers and stilted fucking moans of "I think we belong together, sweetheart," which Benji followed with a primal plea of "Yes, *please*."

William whipped the underwear off Benji's legs before falling between them, perfectly slotting into the home Benji made for him as he opened his thighs. As Benji opened his heart for the long beats of time in which their bodies were moving together, and bliss was searing through his sensitive body, and William was breaking apart, piece by piece, in his arms.

William's orgasm seemed to wash away his reservations, to strip him down to nothing but a wild animal soothed only by Benji's kiss. Benji reached between their bodies, and it was the easiest thing in the world to follow his valentine off the edge of the cliff, to positively splatter William's chest with his come.

The attic bedroom came back to Benji in increments, reaching him through hazy eyes and ringing ears. The flicker of the fire in the wood-burning stove. The scent of sweat and sex and cinnamon candles. William's mouth sucking up kisses along Benji's stomach. The tick of the heater kicking off. The words they had shared.

"Hey," Benji whispered.

William lifted his face. His lips were glossy with Benji's come. Benji pulled William up his body and licked a glob of spunk off his chin. The bright, seaside taste burst on his tongue. William straddled Benji's stomach. Benji stared at William's dick, still sheathed in a condom. It was a super fine dick.

William laughed and cupped Benji's cheek, forcing Benji to look at him. "Go on a date with me."

"Huh?"

William closed his eyes and took a deep breath. "I shouldn't ask you that while we're in our current state. My brain just exploded, and if you're even a smidge as affected, I shouldn't put you on the spot. Let me get your card."

"What is happening right now?"

William rolled out of bed, took care of the condom, and waded through their discarded clothes to find his pants. He pulled a card out of the pocket.

Benji sat up. His body felt a little tender and used. He loved it.

William climbed into Benji's lap and handed the card

over. It was purple. On the cover, William had pasted a pale pink heart and inscribed "My Valentine" within the confines of the heart. Benji flipped the card open. On the inside, William had created a unicorn out of different colors of cardstock. The horn was glittery.

Emotions clogged Benji's throat. In scrolling, pretty cursive, William had written, "A date. Please?"

A date. And maybe that one date would lead to more nights. Nights that would make Benji feel free and courageous and so fucking good.

"Think about it," William said as he brushed his fingers through Benji's hair.

Or maybe it wouldn't. Maybe that date would highlight all the ways Benji and William didn't fit together. The ways Benji didn't fit William's list of hopes and dreams.

The sun woke William the next morning. Benji was spooned against him, snoring quietly and drooling on William's forearm.

The attic bedroom was awash with pink and orange filtering through the big wall of windows. William tensed involuntarily. The house was creaking in a way that indicated people were moving around downstairs. Damn it.

His chest was kind of weak with wanting and tenderness after last night. He wasn't ready to examine it too closely yet. They hadn't spoken about what they'd done or the words that had slipped out in the moment. Benji hadn't said yes or no to the date yet. Last night, William had been hopeful, but in the rosy morning light, he worried his hopefulness had been naivety.

He kissed the back of Benji's neck and tried to move his arm from under Benji without waking him. Benji grabbed William's hand and cuddled it to his chest.

"Are you holding me cuddle hostage, baby?" William asked when it was clear Benji was awake.

Benji made an adorable noise in the back of his throat. "*No* … but it's our last morning."

"It doesn't have to be."

A leaden silence followed William's words, and unease trilled up the back of his neck.

"Thank you," Benji said. "For last night. It was … great, I guess. That word doesn't seem big enough." There was an air of finality in his voice that made William's heart race. It felt like they were dancing around something bad.

"It really doesn't," William agreed. "I want to see you again, Benji. Soon. You know that, don't you?"

Benji rolled over in William's arms and buried his face in William's chest. "My sister set us up."

"What?"

"Sasha. She purposefully didn't tell me the party was postponed. She wanted this, me and you, to happen."

"When did she tell you that?"

"Yesterday."

That mental paradigm shift was a bit of a shock but not necessarily a bad one. "That's … well, that's …" William swallowed. "How do you feel about that?"

Benji shrugged. "Manipulated, mostly. Does it change things?"

William grabbed Benji's cheeks and waited until Benji lifted his gaze. "Not for me. Not at all."

"I'm worried this—*us*—won't be as magical when we leave this house. I'm worried I won't—" Benji shook his head roughly.

"Won't what?"

"Be a good fit for you. Our whole romance has been artificial."

Not for William. He wanted to be a fit for Benji so badly, but there was no denying their differences. Benji was still young and figuring his life out. He might not want to saddle himself with someone like William. And maybe these moony thoughts swirling in William were an emotional high from a Valentine's Day spent together. Maybe William had been so starved for affection for so long that being fed for once made him feel loved.

Or maybe … maybe they were special. *This* was special.

"It's not artificial."

"Isn't it? We were fake secret valentines." Benji laughed. "We basically went to bangtown all weekend. We had rose petals and candlelight and lingerie and endless chocolate. That won't follow us home. It's not real."

The cloying taste of panic bloomed on the back of William's tongue. This could not be the end, but he wasn't sure how to explain himself.

"It is real," William managed. "To me." He pressed Benji's palm to his chest.

"Your heart is beating fast."

"Yeah, I feel like you're breaking up with me."

A small smile teased the edges of Benji's mouth. "I don't know what I'm doing. Here. Anywhere. I'm a mess."

"You're not a mess." *You're amazing*, William wanted to say but didn't have the guts. "Give me a chance. A date. If you're uncertain after that date, you never have to see me again. You can even bail on the Bachelorian Auction."

Some light returned to Benji's eyes, but his smile was reserved. "You are the best valentine. One date." He nodded as if that settled it.

They stayed in bed for another hour, sharing kisses that belied the end of their romantic weekend.

When they surfaced, the whole crew was having coffee on the dock. They cheered as William and Benji joined them. William's cheeks went hot in the chilly air. Guess the cat was finally out of the bag.

"Oh hush," William said.

"No, keep going. Shower me in praise and attention, please," Benji teased. His sister caught him in a hug before turning it into a noogie.

William listened to his favorite people in the world laugh at his and Benji's expense and felt an overwhelming sense of love in his heart. He was surrounded by his friends. Loved by them. People he'd taken for granted for far too long.

Wren—his best friend, his kindred match.

Robin—the most thoughtful, intentional person he knew.

Avi—his moody college roommate with a heart of gold.

Manuel—the sunshine in every room, a man who brought out the best in everyone who crossed his path, including his husband.

Perry—a new addition to their weekend away, but he looked at Sasha like the world began and ended with her, which was good enough for William.

Sasha—bold, funny, raunchy, the life of every party, the only person who could successfully get him drunk.

And Benji. Beautiful Benji. Amazing Benji.

Benji with a secret folder of photos on his phone. Benji who smelled like watermelon because of body wash *and* kitchen disasters.

Benji with messy hair and an ornery smile and freckles on his nose and big, bottomless blue eyes that were lit up with laughter.

Benji who didn't think they fit together. Benji who would be proven wrong.

Benji. Just fuck. Benji.

Chapter Nineteen

It had been three days since Benji had said goodbye to William at the lake house. Three days of worry and second-guessing. Three days of picturing William's stupid list of criteria when he closed his eyes, and three days of missing William with his whole heart.

And it had only been two hours since William had picked Benji up for their date. Two hours of hell.

Maybe mercury was in retrograde. Benji had seen a drag queen tweeting about that today. There had to be some explanation for how horribly this date was going.

They'd started with drinks at a place called Sky Bar at the Plaza. It was on the fortieth floor of a building downtown. Benji had ordered the cheapest glass of wine on the menu (at a whopping and ridiculous twelve dollars). He hadn't been dressed nice enough because he'd not been expecting to go somewhere so fancy.

A bar on the top of a skyscraper with stupidly pricey wine and business-professional clientele was not

Benji's world. He had never before felt so out of his element.

Then at dinner, at a restaurant tagged as very expensive on Yelp (Benji had checked), the server had dropped William's spaghetti in his lap.

While leaving the parking lot, William's car got a flat tire.

The real world did not seem to be on their side, and Benji's fears about the shine wearing off once they left the lake house threatened to choke him. William was still wonderful and hot as sin, but there was no denying this disaster.

Benji tried not to scream over the sidewall gash in the rear wheel tire of William's stupid Alfa as they examined the damage.

Mercury in retrograde. It had to be a thing.

Now William was glaring down at the tire as if his stare could magic it better.

"It's a run-flat," Benji said. "You can drive on the tire for a few miles." Benji hated run-flats. He'd rather just fix a flat and get on with it.

William nodded and took a deep breath. It was cold and drizzly outside. Sprinkles beaded on William's glasses. In the mid-February chill, he looked like a Rolex model standing next to his dumb fancy car wearing a dumb fancy suit and shiny shoes. There was an air of untouchableness to him—even with a plate of pasta staining his slacks—and Benji didn't know how to make that distance disappear or if he should try.

"I was going to take you to a queer burlesque show

uptown," William said. He pulled Benji in front of him and smiled, his hands like anchors on Benji's hips.

And damn, but a burlesque show actually sounded fun. It was *actually* in Benji's wheelhouse, as opposed to everything else they'd done thus far. "That's not going to happen."

William sighed. "Guess not."

"This tire is gonna suck to replace."

"Why?"

"They're expensive as fuck."

"Oh." William frowned and waved his hand. "It's nothing."

A slick prickle of disquiet swept down Benji's spine. They were so different. Those awful bullet points flitted through his brain again.

Bad brain. Evil brain, but Benji couldn't ignore the impulse of self-preservation, hot and metallic on his tongue.

"You shouldn't drive on a damaged tire like this for longer than necessary. Is my apartment between here and your place? I wouldn't want you to have to go out of your way to take me home."

Something flashed in William's eyes—surprise, maybe. Or hurt at the slam of the door on their night.

Benji rushed on, "You should bring this baby to your dealership first thing tomorrow morning."

"Yeah. I can take you home. You ready?" William smiled pleasantly, but his expression harkened back to that muted blank canvas when he'd first opened the door to an unexpected Benji at the lake.

"Yep."

William drove Benji to his apartment, caution lights blinking. They didn't really speak. It took forever because William couldn't drive over thirty miles per hour. Benji squirmed uncomfortably in the senselessly comfortable front seat. He'd never hated an Alfa Romeo Giulia more.

When William reached Benji's apartment, he threw the car into park and turned toward Benji.

"I know this date didn't exactly go as planned," William said.

"No. Not exactly."

"You seem upset."

It was a bit of a shock to realize that William was right. Benji *was* upset. He had been trying to push the emotion down, telling himself that it was silly and immature and self-absorbed to be so disappointed in their evening. This had felt like a test of their mettle, and they'd failed.

"I wanted it to be good." Benji stared out the front windshield. "I wanted to be good for you."

"Hey. You were great, and I don't want you to be anyone but yourself."

"I found your list," Benji said impulsively. "Your 'Prospective Partner Criteria.' I saw it when I came to pull you out of your office on Saturday morning. It was on the top of your bookshelf. I'm not that person, William. I'm like the opposite of that person."

The blood drained from William's face. "Oh."

"Yeah." Benji laughed, but it wasn't funny. "I don't want to try to change who I am to appease a guy. Never again. But I also want you to have the partner you deserve."

"Wait. Hold on. I'm trying to remember what I wrote on that list. I've hardly thought about it since I met you."

"You want someone who is older and rich and boring." Damn, but Benji was feeling bitchy about that.

William stared for a beat before a shocked laugh burst forth. "No. I want you. I was writing that list when you showed up. Within three hours, do you know what I was thinking? *Benji* is my list. I want someone who back-talks and teases. Someone who challenges me and makes me laugh. Someone who is dirty and sweet and complex and earthy as fuck."

Panic blared through Benji. This was exactly what he'd wanted to hear, but his brain wasn't ready for it. He shook his head, as if he was saying, "No, no, no."

William continued, his voice strident now. "Within a day, I was thinking that I needed to add a bullet point about sunrises and a bullet point about the scent of watermelon and a bullet point about grease under your fingernails. And you and you and you. I want you. That list is nothing."

"It didn't feel like nothing to me. Not when I found it and didn't match a single fucking criterion, William," Benji spit out. "We just had a DEFCON disaster date. And even without the spilled spaghetti and even without the flat tire and aborted plans, you took me to the fanciest bar in the entire world and ordered a twenty-five-dollar glass of wine, and I couldn't think of anything to talk about, and I felt *so stupid* and—"

"Hey. Whoa," William said, cupping the side of Benji's neck. "I'm sorry. You're right. I wanted to take you somewhere fancy, but I misjudged. I'm not in my element at those places either."

"I had to Google things on the menu at the restaurant. I had no idea what half the stuff was."

William laughed, and Benji's stomach dropped.

"Why do you think I ordered the spaghetti?" William said.

Had Benji completely misread everything tonight? He bumped his head against the back of the headrest. He'd never been this mortified on a date, and he'd had his fair share of shitty ones.

"Sweetheart," William said. "Look at me."

Benji did, his heart rebelling at William's gentle tone.

"Remember when we talked about love? And you said you thought it'd be big billboards. Do you remember what I said?"

Benji gazed into William's eyes. "Yeah, I do." He'd said that love was in the small disasters.

"Tonight, when the waitress dropped my plate, I thought, 'This is as funny as when Benji knocked the watermelon off the counter,' and 'I can't wait to laugh about this with him later.' When the tire blew, I thought, 'God, I love his eyes,' and 'I hope he teases me about this.'"

"Ugh, I feel like a dick now."

"You're not a dick."

Benji's brain was going to explode. He'd been so prepared for this to go poorly that it was as if he'd created a self-fulfilling prophecy. Maybe he'd doomed them to a bad date by not having faith.

But it was hard to have faith when so many people had rejected him and stifled his self-expression.

"That list wasn't nothing to me," Benji said again, trying, yet failing, to explain.

William brushed his fingers through Benji's hair. "I don't need you to be anyone but yourself."

Want versus need. Benji sucked in a shuddery breath. He opened his mouth to speak, but William got there first.

"What I'm offering is my heart," William said. "The whole thing. Because the little disasters with you have been better than just about anything I've ever experienced."

Damn. Benji swallowed hard. He felt like he couldn't breathe. "This has been moving so fast, and I'm feeling so much. It's a lot. I think I need some time to think about us."

He was retreating, and he knew it wasn't the right thing to do, but everything about tonight had confused him, in good and bad ways. He needed a moment to put himself back together.

William nodded, disappointment clear on his face, but he leaned over the center console and kissed Benji softly. "Will I still see you Saturday?"

"What's Saturday?"

"The Bachelorian Auction," William said.

"Oh. I'd forgotten."

William smiled, but it was more of a grimace. "Don't

worry about it. Come if you want. If you don't, that's okay, but a second date—think about that, please."

The next morning, Benji texted his sisters: *Emergency brunch. A.S.A.P.*

Benji got there early. Rosie was the next to show. Also early. She was always prompt.

Today she was wearing a prim purple sweater and a plaid skirt. Her hair was pulled back with a ribbon. She was cool as a cucumber.

Born fourteen months apart, Rosie and Sasha were often mistaken for twins. They both had pixie faces and fine blonde hair and expressive blue eyes, but Rosie was rational and reticent, where Sasha was brash and wild.

"How was your date?" Benji asked. He wanted to hear about billiards guy.

She folded her hands over her lap. "He got drunk during dinner, flirted with the waitress, told me my divorce was my fault, then cried about the one-who-got-away. I never want to date again."

"Holy saints of courtly love," Benji cursed. "What a fuckboy. Also, your divorce was not your fault, Ro. Voldemort was a disloyal, lying, self-absorbed grease stain. He was a seeping bedsore. He—"

She smiled wanly and waved her hand. "I'm fine. I don't want to talk about me. Are you okay? Sasha told me you slept with William O'Dare, which I have to admit, I did not see coming."

Ah, there was that oldest-sibling syndrome Benji had been missing.

Their trusty regular waitress delivered a pitcher of mimosas to the table without having to ask if they wanted it. She had their order down pat.

Benji helped himself. "What do you think of William?" he asked, not answering Rosie's initial question. He had no idea if he was okay. He was all shaken up inside.

"He works too hard."

Benji laughed. "Do you like him? I like him." He took a deep breath. "I think he likes me."

She tapped a perfectly manicured fingernail on the table. "I should hope so, considering you spent an entire weekend in his bed."

"Liking someone has not been a prerequisite for me to spend a weekend in their bed and vice versa."

She reached across the syrup-sticky table and grabbed his hand. "It's about damn time to change that, sweet pea."

He nodded, heat burning his eyes. "Yeah. I went on a date with him."

"Oh really?" she said, a bit of teasing slipping into her dry voice. "And how was that?"

"Pretty bad, actually. But maybe also very good. Can I ask you a question about love? It's okay if you don't want to talk about it. It might push some divorce buttons."

She rolled her eyes. "Go on."

"How do you think love is supposed to feel?"

"Are you in love with William?" she asked, alarmed.

Now it was his turn to roll his eyes. "Of course not. We just met. But how will I know? How will I know to trust it?"

She bit her bottom lip. "Shit, I need something stronger than a mimosa."

"We don't have to talk about it."

He watched as Rosie constructed a wall around her emotions. Her face went mostly blank. "I've been in love twice. Once with Landon, of course."

"The devil."

She ignored him. "But the first time I fell in love, I was seventeen."

"With who?"

She waved her hand. "Doesn't matter. We broke up after graduation. With my husband, love was consuming and breath-stealing and wild. I couldn't think rationally or behave myself. I didn't like how it made me feel or act, but I couldn't stop it either. The first time I fell in love, in high school, it was quieter. Different. There was more affection and discovery and wonder. I felt like *myself* but the best version of myself. It didn't hurt me to love him. It didn't tear me down or break me into consumable pieces. It did the opposite."

Benji nodded, enthralled by Rosie's words. She was normally not so emotive or open.

"Love is an individual thing. It can be big or small or consuming or a breath of fresh air. It depends," she concluded.

What Benji wanted was a love that didn't try to

change him or break him down, as Rosie had put it. William had never asked him to change, but Benji had kept him at arm's length out of fear, insecurity, and self-preservation. At some point, Benji had to trust other people to hold his heart with care, and frankly, he'd never met anyone as worthy of trust as William.

Benji wanted a love that made him his best self, that existed in the small moments—the flat tires and the awkward conversations—as well as the big ones, like on a bed of rose petals or a stage in front of everyone.

A stage in front of everyone.

"Oh shit. I know what I need to do," he said.

Rosie smiled wryly.

A sudden din made them both jump. Sasha had dropped her purse and coat next to Benji before plopping into the booth beside Rosie.

"Hiya," Sasha said. She stole Benji's mimosa and downed it in one go. "What is our emergency brunch topic today?"

Benji glanced at Rosie and grinned. "Don't worry. I think I've got it settled."

Chapter Twenty

The Bach Auction had come together with a bang. William's business partner was running interference to ensure it went smoothly, and he was staying out of her way. He was the numbers guy. She was the people person. She liked it when he stayed out of her way.

But right now, he wished he was busy. His heart was beating fast. He was sweaty. He felt awkward posted up at the bar by himself, and he was scared Benji wouldn't show. The auction was already underway, the dance floor busy with bidding, and William hadn't seen any sign of him.

He was scared he'd never see Benji again, honestly.

Robin collapsed onto the barstool beside him and signaled to the bartender for a beer. She'd told him she'd be there to watch Wren get auctioned off. "Sorry I'm late. The club looks amazing."

"It does." His voice was tight. "I'm really proud of the crew here."

"You should be proud of yourself. This is special."

The Auction was themed Sweet and Sickening and had been advertised as a post-Valentine's Day bash for sexy—and charitable-minded—singles.

The stage had white-and-purple-striped sashing around the edges, and the backdrop was Pepto-Bismol pink. Mixed in with the sugary colors were slashes of black and severe dark green—an incongruence that was oddly appealing. The lighting turned the whole dance floor an eerie cotton-candy blue and huge fake conversation hearts hung from the ceiling with phrases like "Swipe Left" and "Not Today, Satan" and "Suck My Tits."

It had been his five-year plan to move into the queer-spaces market, and he was incredibly happy with this, his first venture, more so today than any other day.

"Thanks. I am proud."

"So, you and Benji Holiday. What's the deal there, stud?" Robin asked, her voice teasing. "Have you seen him since last weekend?"

"We went on a date, but I, and the universe, ruined it." He rotated on his stool to face her. "He thinks he isn't the type of person I want long term."

A cheer went up from the crowd in reaction to activity on the stage, but they both ignored it.

Her brow furrowed. "Is he?"

"Yes. If he wants me."

"Sounds like you've got to win him back, then." Robin grinned and the club lights sparkled in her deep brown eyes. "What could you do? Oh, write him a poem."

William laughed. "No."

"A song?"

"No."

"It needs to be something big."

A bell dinged in his head. It did need to be something big. For Benji, it should be big. "You're right."

"He has brunch with his sisters once a week," Robin said.

"Yes." William nodded, on a roll. "I could show up there wearing pajamas, with a huge bouquet of roses that he's just going to tear apart to scatter somewhere, and I could get up on the diner counter and—"

"Why pajamas?" Robin asked.

William couldn't meet Robin's eyes. "Benji liked me in pajamas. Pajamas are a great equalizer. Everyone looks ridiculous in them."

Rosie covered her mouth with her hand. "You are so gone for him. I don't think I realized. Oh, speak of the devil."

William spun around, hoping to see Benji, only to find Sasha, Rosie, and Wren swimming through the crowd to sidle up to them. Wren immediately ordered shots when she reached the bar.

Wren had been one of the first bachelorians, and he hadn't seen her since she'd stepped off the stage. She had evidently been partying it up with the Holiday sisters.

"Hi ladies," he said. Then turning to Sasha, he asked, "Have you talked to Benji in the last few days?" Maybe he could mine her for information.

Sasha shook her head. "Not really. He didn't want to

come out with us tonight. Said he was busy, so we made it a girls' night!"

Disappointment pummeled William. He'd been holding out hope that Benji would be here, but it seemed like avoidance was Benji's plan instead.

"You defiled my baby brother," Rosie said, slightly slurry but with an impish smile.

William's mouth dropped. He hadn't seen Rosie in over a year, but she was typically very reserved.

"To be fair, I don't think I did much with Benji that he hadn't done before." That wasn't quite true though. They had done plenty that was new and exciting for both of them.

"I'm drunk," Rosie said. She was wearing denim on denim with a bandana headband and bright red lipstick that was slightly smeared.

"I can see that."

"I'm glad you're a good guy. So many guys aren't."

Sasha laughed and grabbed her sister around the waist. "Okay, sis. Let's cool the drunken earnestness for a few minutes."

A local drag queen named Ms. Gena Ross was introducing a new bachelorian on the stage, to the hoots and hollers of the audience, so William's attention was diverted. This bach was a teacher who enjoyed playing chess, competing in drag king competitions, and watching cartoons. She was offering up five hours of personal Spanish language classes.

Once bidding started, William waved to the

bartender. A few minutes later, the bartender plopped a manhattan down in front of him.

"Sasha, what day do you and Rosie usually have brunch with Benji?" William asked during a lull.

She shrugged. "Depends on his work schedule. Why?"

Robin laughed into her drink.

William said, "No reason."

The crowd on the dance floor cheered as bidding ended on the teacher. They were using this cool bidding app, and the bids were transmitted onto a huge screen by the stage. All the audience had to do was press a button on their phone to increase their bid.

William lifted his glass to his lips as Ms. Gena Ross said, "And our next sexy single is a hot-ass mechanic. Everyone give a big gay welcome to Benji Holidaaaamn."

Benji marched out on stage. He was wearing jeans, combat boots, and a black sheer tank top that showed the pink harness underneath. The glass in William's hand slipped from his fingers, sloshing his drink over the sleeve of his Henley. He caught the glass before it spun onto the floor.

Benji Holiday, standing proud on that Candyland stage, completely knocked William apart.

"Benji is a pretty boy who likes to get his hands dirty," Ms. Gena Ross said. "He knows the best automotive lubricants and isn't afraid to use them. In addition to being real fabulous at changing your oil, Benji enjoys pancakes, college basketball, and all things lace." Ms. Gena glanced down at the notecard in her hand and back at him. "You are a study in contradictions, honey bun."

Benji laughed, his face noticeably rosy, and William's heart seemed to launch toward him.

Ms. Gena Ross continued, "Why don't you tell your adoring fans what you have on offer, big guy? I have it on good authority that it's a bit special." She handed the mic to Benji.

Benji shuffled his feet, all aw-shucks cuteness in his shit-hot harness, and took the mic from her.

"Hi, everyone," Benji said, his voice wavering. William stood. He wanted to rush up there and soothe him. "I'm offering an oil and filter change, but I don't want anyone to bid on me. Well, except one person. Don't worry. He's rich. He can afford me. His car sucks to service too, so I'm kind of a steal."

The crowd laughed, and William's breath snagged in his throat.

Benji continued on. "William O'Dare, a week ago, we talked about love and relationships and finding our perfect matches. I said I thought love was big gestures and explosions and billboards. You said it was in the small stuff. I think it might be both. I want the small stuff with you. The little disasters. The flat tires, the lost keys, the sick days ... the power outages. But you also deserve the grand gestures because you're kind and generous and accepting and so fucking hot."

William pressed a hand to his rabbiting heartbeat.

Benji met his eye over the heads of the crowd. "This is a grand gesture for you, by the way. Was that clear?"

William yelled, "Yes!" An impulsive, untamed happiness burst through his chest.

Benji grinned. "I trust you. I want you to be my valentine for a bit longer. Like, a lot longer." He handed the microphone back to Ms. Gena Ross to much whistling and cheering.

"Well, smack my ass and call me Cherry. I was not expecting that," Gena said. "Since William O'Dare owns this fucking club, and I suspect he can afford it, I say we start the bidding at one hundred dollars? And so help me God, if any of y'all monsters bid, I'll chuck Benji off the stage at you."

William rushed toward the stage. The crowd split and made room. He jogged up the steps to the stage. Benji grinned at him. He had sweat beading in the notch of his throat and a flush high on his cheekbones.

"I was planning a grand gesture for *you*. You beat me to the punch!" William laughed, joy almost overwhelming him.

"Really?"

"Yes, really. It involved brunch."

Benji smiled shyly. "I have something for you." He pushed a slightly wrinkled, homemade card into William's hand. William's heart felt raw and exposed.

It was not a pretty card. There were candy hearts glued inside it, but they made the card heavy and awkward. Two hearts had fallen off and left behind bubbles of superglue.

William loved it.

"I'd been wondering what you were making with these candy hearts." The candy was glued in the shape of what he guessed was supposed to be an anatomically correct heart with an arrow piercing it. Benji had written William's name on the inside of the heart in bubble letters.

"They're called Sweethearts," Benji said.

"What are?"

"The candy hearts. That's the real name. Sweethearts. It's on the bag. You call me sweetheart too."

"I do."

Benji tapped the other side of the card. In pencil was the word "Yes."

"What's the *yes* for?" William asked.

"A second date."

William caught Benji's face in his hands and kissed him. And kissed him. And kissed him.

"Okay, Mister Boss Man, but you still have to bid. It's for charity," Ms. Gena Ross said. William pulled his wallet out of his back pocket and tossed it to her. Then he kissed Benji again.

Epilogue

ONE YEAR LATER

Benji lay back on the dock and stared up at the stars. It had been a mild February. Copper Lake wasn't even frozen.

The stars danced brightly through the sky and a train whistle sounded in the far distance. It was tranquil here in the winter.

He liked coming to William's lake house in the winter more than the summer, he'd found. It had a stark beauty, but he'd never in a million years admit that to William. Benji still referred to it as "your ugly lake" when they made plans to spend time out here, which was basically every weekend that Benji didn't have to work.

William's footsteps thudded on the wooden dock. Benji tipped his head back to watch him approach.

"Hi, sweetheart."

"Hi."

William lay on his back next to Benji and gazed up at the stars too. They linked hands.

Benji lifted William's hand and kissed it. "Did you get your work done?"

William's job was busy, but he didn't let it consume him. He didn't ever sleep in his office. Instead, he slept with Benji, wherever Benji was. Whether they were in Benji's one-bedroom apartment, William's fancy penthouse, or the attic bedroom here at the lake house, they rarely spent a night apart.

"Yeah, and I did the dishes," William said.

"A man after my own heart."

"I know."

Benji laughed and playfully slapped William's stomach. William was wearing a fuzzy sweatshirt. Benji couldn't help but turn and burrow into it.

It was pitch black on the dock but for the stars, and Benji's mind automatically went to whether they could get away with fucking out here. It wasn't too terribly cold. The closest neighbor was directly across the lake, and they only spent the summers here.

William must have been able to read his mind, because he rolled Benji over and said, "Yes."

They wrestled around for long minutes, pulling clothes partially out of the way. After a moment of frustration that he couldn't feel William's cock against his own, Benji sat up abruptly, straddling William's legs.

But they'd somehow moved to the edge of the dock in their shuffle, and Benji overbalanced. He flailed. William tried to grab him, but the momentum knocked Benji for a loop and he tumbled right off the dock into shallow, muddy water. He landed on his side but managed to roll to his hands and knees immediately.

William gasped and stared down at him, his eyes luminous behind his glasses.

"Are you okay?"

The water was only about two feet deep. Benji stood up slowly, mud squelching under his hiking boots. (He was a country boy now—he owned hiking boots.)

"Fine," Benji bit out.

"Can this be one of those little disasters we're always talking about?" William asked, visibly trying to stifle his laughter.

Benji glared and stomped out of the lake, not even trying to crawl back onto the dock, just marched through cattails and dead grass to reach the shore. William caught up with Benji as he made it to the back door. Benji toed off his boots, shucked his sweatpants down, and whipped off his jacket and sweatshirt, throwing the latter at William's face. All the clothes were wet and muddy.

Benji was shivering slightly from the cold, but his skin heated as William stared at him in the starlight. A lamp on in the house cast a square of light onto the ground, but Benji moved away from it, preferring the dark.

William pulled his fuzzy shirt off and gently dropped it over Benji's head, swathing him in it.

Caretaking like that mushed up Benji's insides. Made him pliant and so incredibly happy it hurt.

"I'll get mud on it."

"I don't mind," William said. Then William's lips

were on Benji's neck, on the hollow under his ear, his temple, his chin. His mouth.

Benji let it take him under. He was standing there in nothing but a baby pink cotton thong and a fuzzy sweatshirt. It was cold and he was wet, but this shot up his list of top five ways to spend an evening.

One—having the love of his life slowly strip his thong off and jerk Benji's cock with it wrapped around his hand.

Two—pizza.

No wait.

Two—rim jobs.

William turned Benji until his chest was pressed to the wall of the house, then dropped to his knees behind him. William used the soft cotton of the underwear on Benji's cock, giving him all kinds of textures and pressures.

"Hold yourself open for me, my love."

Heat flared through Benji. He treasured the sweet things William called him. He loved the dirty ones too, but nothing, absolutely nothing, was as wonderful as "my love."

Benji pulled his cheeks apart, and William dove in. The wind rustled the branches of the tree on the side of the house and raised goosebumps on Benji's legs.

William moaned as his tongue painted a stripe up Benji's crack.

"So good," Benji whispered. "You're so good, William."

William fisted Benji's cock, gripping it hard. They'd had a year together to practice this. To learn each other.

To fall more and more in love, and damn, but William was amazing at it.

"Love, oh fuck. I love you," Benji cried out as William thrust his tongue into Benji's hole.

William pulled back. "Do you, now? Is it because I'm awesome at rim jobs?"

They'd started their relationship a year ago with rimming. Felt like they'd come full circle.

Benji laughed breathlessly and turned around, practically tackling William to the ground. William's pants were open from their tussle on the dock. Benji wrenched them down.

William delicately wrapped Benji's thong around the base of both of their cocks, like a loose band, binding them together.

"That's pretty," William said, sounding gut-punched.

"Yeah." Benji spat down onto their cocks, the saliva painting the heads.

"Yes, sweetheart." William spread the wetness over them, helped along by Benji's pre-come.

A few quick tugs, and Benji busted all over William's hand. Benji smothered his cries, his love words, into William's mouth.

William lifted a come-soaked thumb to Benji's bottom lip, smearing Benji's own spunk on his mouth. Benji gulped in a gasping breath and kissed William, sharing the come between them.

William gripped his own prick, using Benji's jizz as lube, and shattered as soon as Benji trailed a finger into the hollow of William's armpit.

Benji laughed. That armpit worked like a trigger. It was amazing.

Then William was laughing too, and they were whispering endearments between them.

Finally, once the trip hammer of their hearts had slowed, William pulled back and said, "Little disasters and huge explosions."

"That's us, huh?"

"Yeah. I love it. Love you." He peppered Benji's face with kisses. "Love you, love you, love you."

Neither of them could stop shaking, their legs were covered in mud, and Benji's thong was probably wrecked for good, which sucked because he'd planned to take a picture in it for his ten thousand Instagram followers.

Benji hugged William and let out a deep, happy sigh. He had never felt so at home. At home with himself, at home with another person.

"I love you too. Happy Valentine's Day," Benji whispered into the sweaty join of William's neck and shoulder.

"In two days."

"Happy Early Valentine's Day," Benji corrected. "This house is going to be overrun by troublemakers tomorrow. I wanted to get the romance in now."

"Well, I have a bubble bath upstairs with your name on it. Happy Early Valentine's Day."

"Make sure to pull the recycling inside. I don't want raccoons to interrupt us again." It was a fairly common occurrence.

"I will. Go on. I'll meet you in our room."

Our room. Benji loved that. Their room. Their love. Their life together.

Benji pressed a gentle, slow kiss to William's lips. Then he slipped William some tongue. At last, Benji whispered, "You're the best valentine ever."

Excerpt from STOCKING STUFFERS (So
Over the Holidays #1)

Did you miss the first book in the So Over the Holiday series? Read on for Chapter 1 of *Stocking Stuffers*!

Sasha lifted the toy from her huge red bag with a flourish, and the jingle bells on her reindeer antlers tinkled merrily.

"This little darling, the Love Bite, is my favorite of the bunch." She displayed the toy in her hands like a model on *The Price is Right*. She'd found, after years of peddling her wares to anyone and everyone who would listen, that drama sells. Especially at Christmas. "The handle is ergonomic, and it's sturdy. Frankly, there is nothing I hate more than a flimsy sex toy."

The Staunchly Raunchy Book Club members tittered, and Sasha grinned. "Y'all know what I mean. I can tell."

Gently teasing the clients was one of Sasha's customer

service tricks. She was adept at figuring out which Lady Robin's Intimate Implements partygoers were gregarious and bantering with them. But today, Sasha's heart wasn't exactly full of holiday cheer *or* consumerism. She felt like the fake elf at the party, and she'd never been a very good faker.

"The Love Bite uses suction technology, and I swear to the Ghost of Good Orgasms Past, it's the closest to real oral I've ever found in a sex toy. You just place the head over your clit and it creates a suck-and-release sensation," she said matter-of-factly.

Sasha normally loved filling in at a Lady Robin's sales party when one of the regular reps called in sick. She loved chatting with the clients, and she definitely loved the commission money.

But she *hated* Christmas, so this party sucked.

Sasha passed the Love Bite to Valerie, the party's hostess and a beautiful femme lesbian, who tested the suction on her thumb.

"Oh, very nice," Valerie said. "I might give up the girlfriend search for this baby." She waved the Love Bite at her friends. "This is my new girlfriend now!"

Sasha couldn't hold in her professional pride. "Plus, it's waterproof."

Sasha's friend, Robin, had started Lady Robin's Intimate Implements, a boutique sex toy and lingerie company, as a pop-up shop seven years ago. Sasha had been the whole of the marketing department for the first three years before their company had exploded into a multi-city operation. They supplemented their online and local vendor sales with bridal showers and birthday parties attended by their salaried marketing reps. This was the first book club they'd been commissioned for, as far as Sasha knew. Their company had made Robin, and Sasha by extension, stockings full of cash.

A blast of wind hit the Winterberry Inn, causing the old house to creak and rattle. Sasha whipped around to see out the big bay window. It was dark out there, and she desperately hoped the expected snow and ice held off until she was home. Her darling baby—a restored 1984 VW Bug—was a disaster on icy roads.

Valerie, who owned the Winterberry Inn and was definitely the evil mastermind of the Staunchly Raunchy Book Club, called a pause on the proceedings to get everyone mulled wine and spiked eggnog. Sasha took the brief reprieve to glance around the luxurious hearth room. The inn was a cozy bed and breakfast with seemingly endless rooms and Christmas charm in every nook and cranny.

The hearth room spilled over with Christmas bobbles, garland, boxwood wreaths, and lights. A huge spruce tree, decked out in glittery gold, was activating Sasha's allergies.

Christmas made her itch, even when it was beautiful.

Maybe especially when it was beautiful.

Once the book club members were back in their circle of seats, Sasha pulled a paddle out of her bag and pasted on a fake smile.

"We don't have a huge variety of impact-play instruments, like crops or whips, but if you're in the market for that, I can give you suggestions for other vendors. We only have one paddle, but it's exceptional, if I do say so myself." She brandished the wooden paddle Robin had created for the holidays. It had a word etched into the wide, flat end. "You can personalize the word, so it could be your name or your partner's name. Other common words are *BABY* or *SLUT*. This is our Christmas edition, you know, if Santa gets you going."

The group laughed as she handed off the paddle adorned with the word *HO!* The book club members had been discussing a BDSM romance novel when she'd arrived, and the group erupted in chatter as they deliberated over whether the characters in the book would have enjoyed such play.

Sounded like they definitely would have been down.

Sasha listened to them with half an ear as she removed the last items from her bag. For a perverse second, she wished her roller bag was velvet, like Santa's, rather than boring nylon. Velvet would match the red dress she'd donned in the hopes of appearing to be a bundle of cheer.

False cheer, but whatever.

Once the room quieted down, Sasha displayed her final toys.

"Last but not least, next month we're debuting a new line called Prick Me, for the person or persons in your life with dicks and prostates, but we have a bit of stock available for purchase today. Call it a sexy sneak peek."

She waved one of the toys—a holly-green cylinder with an opening on one end. "Here is our Fancy Flesh-stroker, which comes in twelve diverse skin tones and several fun colors. These have a soft, silky interior and are super easy to clean. We're also debuting two vibrating prostate massagers of differing shapes, named, quite simply, the P-Spot Pulse and Pulse 2."

She held them up and demonstrated how to turn them both on.

A quiet, earnest-looking white woman named Louise laughed. "This might sound stupid, but can you explain how those work?"

Sasha smiled, a real one this time, and put her proverbial sex-educator cap on. "So the prostate is a gland in front of the rectum in people born with penises and prostates. It has tons of pleasure sensors, so it can feel good when it's stimulated. A lot of people with prostates enjoy having theirs touched, and that isn't specific to certain sexualities. Prostate play can result in some pretty spectacular orgasms. With consent, of course, all you have to do is lube this baby up and insert it into——"

A big *thump* resounded almost directly behind her, and she dropped the toys onto the hardwood floor. Somehow, the vibrator on the Pulse 2 was activated on impact, so it buzzed and danced all over the place.

As she scrambled down to grab the toy, trying not to flash everyone since her holiday dress was *short*, Valerie shouted, "Perry! What are you doing here?"

Sasha got the toy turned off before twisting around. There was a man standing in the entryway of the room, a gym bag—evidently full of bricks considering the noise it had made when hitting the ground—by his feet.

Hot damn.

He was the type of man who could make her Christmas knickers twist. Tall, lean, pale, with dark curly hair and a beard. Plus, he was staring at her like she was a piece of rum cake.

She wanted to be his rum cake.

Double damn.

He ran a hand roughly through his hair. "I drove in a day early to beat the winter storm, which didn't work. It's already icy out there. I didn't expect to walk in on my favorite book club getting a sex-toy demo." He didn't take his eyes off Sasha.

Chuckles filled the room, and Sasha slowly stood up. No one seemed particularly perturbed about being interrupted by this man. Instead, the room was alight with excitement at his arrival. She smoothed her red velvet dress down with one hand while clutching the sex toys in the other. Her stupid antlers jingled.

Valerie waved an arm dismissively. "Well, you showed up a day early, so …"

"So?" He was still staring at Sasha, his gaze tracking over her face.

"So maybe it's your own fault if your delicate constitution can't handle talk of prostate massagers," Sasha said with an extra dose of sass.

A grin slowly spread across his face, and dear God, he was hotter than she'd realized.

"Fair assessment. I'm sorry, we've never met. I'm Perry Winters." He finally drew his attention away from her and checked out the members of the Staunchly

Raunchy Book Club. "I think I know all the other Raunchies here, but not you."

Raunchies? Was that what they called themselves? Because that was adorable.

He stuck his hand out, and Sasha stumbled on her way over to shake it. His hand was sturdy and huge. Occasionally, Sasha loved the feel of soft, delicate hands, but Perry was making her crave large, strong, and callused.

"Sasha, and I'm just the sex-toy marketeer."

His eyes darkened deliciously at that. "I doubt you're *just* anything."

"Perry's my brother," Valerie said. "He used to be in our book club before he moved to Topeka, like a dweeb."

His hand began to slip from Sasha's, and she jerked her palm from his. They'd held on too long. "You were in *this* book club?" she asked. He was one of the Raunchies?

"Yes. I like to read," he said, as if it were that simple.

Which, really, *it was*.

"That's awesome," she said. *And sexy.* She kept that part to herself.

"Hey Perry, have you read the newest Minnesota Motorcycle Club book?" asked Andie, a petite black woman. She was wearing an ugly Christmas sweater with kittens on the front and had slapped a nametag on her chest that said, *Holiday Pussy*. Sasha wanted to be her best friend.

Perry smiled warmly. "I haven't. I DNF'ed the last one, but maybe I'll give the new one a shot," he said.

Most of that went over Sasha's head, so she returned

to her seat and sat primly, waiting for the group to calm down again. After the excitement of Perry's arrival wore off, Sasha looked to Valerie to see if she could continue.

"Right! Sorry, Sasha. We'll let you wrap up, then we'll dive into our game of Dirty Book Dirty Santa."

"Sounds good." Sasha eyed Perry, who'd pulled a folding chair into the circle and was watching her, unconcerned.

It wouldn't be the first time she'd hand-sold sex toys to men, but he made her skin prickle. Made her feel squirmy and excited all at once.

She cleared her throat. "As I was saying, here are our prostate massagers. Use lube."

She directed that last comment at Perry. Rosiness rushed up his cheeks above the line of his beard as he smiled. A blusher. Mayday, too cute for words!

Without stopping to swoon, she continued, "I've also got a catalog for lingerie and underthings that you're welcome to peruse. Our lingerie is size and gender inclusive with a select range of bras, garters, slips, undies, binders, compression gaffs, and strap-on bottoms, all with Lady Robin's rock-and-roll flair. Now, does anyone have any questions?"

Louise raised her hand timidly.

"Yes?"

Louise bit her lip and glanced at Perry. He was a former Raunchy, so they were probably used to him being present, but Louise was obviously not comfortable asking this question in front of him.

Perry stood up abruptly. "Oh man, that eggnog smells

amazing. I'll be back." He rushed toward the breakfast room where the food and drinks were set up. With a smile, Sasha watched his long legs and tight ass waltz from the room.

He was a blusher *and* considerate of women's feelings. She wanted a bite.

Once he was gone, Louise laughed. "Gosh, sorry. I couldn't ask this in front of him. Do you have anything in double-F sizing?"

"Definitely. Everything, including our bralettes."

A few other book club members had questions about sizing and prices as well. As Sasha answered, another huge gust of wind made the house shudder and the lights flicker. She needed to hurry so she could get home before the roads were too treacherous for her Bug.

"Here are the order forms. I have some stock with me today, but if I don't have what you want, we guarantee its arrival in five business days anywhere in the continental US. Feel free to check out the items on display. If no one has any questions, I'm going to run to the restroom real quick."

Valerie directed Sasha to the closest bathroom in a hallway off the huge, gorgeous kitchen, which was also decorated with all manner of garland and Christmas candles. There was a centerpiece made of a grapevine wreath, red garden roses, and berries on the kitchen island. Sasha stopped and stared at it, her heartbeat in her throat.

It was eerily similar to the centerpieces she'd made a year ago for her wedding, only a lot fancier. Like a gut punch, it halted her in her tracks. Blood suddenly thundered in her ears, and her stomach pitched, a metallic taste hitting the back of her tongue. She had to squelch the urge to swipe the centerpiece off the counter and hurried out of the room instead.

Once Sasha was alone in the hallway, she leaned against the wall and tried to slow the frantic patter of her heartbeat. Her phone buzzed in her hand, which was more effective in distracting her than the deep breathing.

It was a weather alert. They were in a Blizzard Warning.

Fucking great.

She also had a text message from her older sister, Rosie.

Rosie: *Roads are horrible on the west side of city. Hope you're not out being wild.*

Sasha: *I'm wrapping up a Lady Robin's party. Will leave soon.*

Rosie was a worrier and a pessimist. Sasha was sure their little brother, Benji, had received a similar message.

Rosie: *Who the hell plans a sex toy party right before X-mas? You need to get home now!*

A laugh worked its way out of Sasha's throat, surprising her.

Sasha: *The dirtiest and coolest book club ever, that's who. Sex toys make the best stocking stuffers.*

Rosie: *Very funny.*

Sasha: *I am. I'll text when I leave. This place is out in the boonies, so I have at least an hour drive to get home.*

It wasn't really the boonies. There were plenty of

other properties around, but to a city girl like Sasha, it might as well have been the great frontier.

"Sasha?"

She jumped at Perry's deep voice and bobbled her phone until it slithered through her fingers and skittered across the floor. Thank God for super-protective cases.

"*Baby Jesus!* Stop making me drop things."

"Sorry. I didn't mean to startle you."

He swooped down and picked up her cell phone. Their fingers brushed when he handed it back, and she shivered. He smelled of cedar.

She liked it. A lot.

Maybe he was a lumberjack. He *was* wearing flannel.

He smiled, his eyes bright. "I feel like I crashed your sales pitch. I'm sorry if I made it awkward."

"Don't worry. I'm not shy."

His gaze landed on her lips before jerking away. "I think half the book club is heading out soon, and the rest are staying at the inn to wait out the storm. They're drawing names for a book exchange rather than playing Dirty Santa."

"Oh, that's good. I'll go get their orders, so I can head home too."

He took a deep breath. "This might be out of line but would you go to dinner with me sometime this week?"

Her pulse galloped off like a herd of reindeer. She hadn't been on a *date* date in ages. Dates led to expectations and crossed boundaries. She hadn't dated since … well, since the worst Christmas ever had soured the idea of relationships for her forever. Being left at the altar on Christmas Eve did that to you.

Rather than spill her issues on an unsuspecting hot guy, she said, "A date? All you know about me is that I sell sex toys for a living."

Some people thought that made her available or even a slut.

"No. I know you're smart and confident, and I like your voice. There's this lilt when you speak, like you're always having a great time and everything is funny. And your hair. I like your hair."

"Wow. Thank you."

A few of her regular lovers had not been fans of her hair when she'd chopped it into a pixie cut a few months ago. Needless to say, they weren't her lovers anymore.

He ran an unsteady hand across his chin and lips. In the darkness of the hallway, she couldn't see his eyes clearly. She wondered what color they were, wanted to see them alight with pleasure. She had a feeling Perry would be delightfully expressive and genuine in bed.

"I'm not the best at this," he said, voice shaky.

"You're actually doing pretty awesome."

"Really?"

"Yeah, really, but I'm not the dating type. And regard-less, don't you live in Topeka?"

His smile withered, and she had the irrational urge to cup his cheek.

What was happening to her?

She wanted to blame her sudden soppy, sweet feelings on the Christmas cheer in the air. It was like those parasitic spores that latched onto everything, multiplied, then smothered their host.

"I *did* live in Topeka. I, uh, I'm not … My living situation is complicated."

"I'm not in the market for complicated," she said. "Though, you're super cute, so I'd probably be game for a night together. A one-night stand, basically. But not tonight because, you know, snow and ice and rear-wheel drive. I need to get home."

His mouth had gone a little slack, and she inwardly cringed. She tended to steamroll people. Men especially expected her to be more circumspect about her sexual appetites and romantic boundaries, but that wasn't her problem. It was theirs.

"I'm sorry. I can't tell if you're rejecting me or propositioning me," he finally said. The corners of his eyes crinkled.

"Both."

"I like you," he said decisively, and she laughed.

"I'm a bit much, I've been told. I like to fuck, eat, masturbate, and read, and I don't do any of those in moderation. Still interested?"

She had no idea why she was unleashing all her sass on him. Maybe to scare him off. Or to see if he'd stick around.

"I'm definitely still interested, Sasha."

Farm College Series

Controlled Burn

Clean Break

Love Life Series

Life on Pause

Life of Bliss

Storm Chasers Series

Natural Disaster

So Over the Holidays Series

Stocking Stuffers

Acknowledgments

This series has given me the ability to write the fun, raunchy, heartfelt, earnest books of my heart. I want to thank everyone who read and enjoyed *Stocking Stuffers*, as well as my other books. Your support has allowed me to continue this series and write *Candy Hearts*.

A big thanks to Edie Danford for her awesome editing, Susie Selva for her thorough proofreading, Cate Ashwood for a kickass and sexy cover, Judith at A Novel Take PR and Leslie at LesCourt for great promo, and my beta readers (and blurb helpers)—Allison, Lisa, Layla, and Karen—for being the best sounding boards.

Extra hugs and kisses to my family.

About the Author

Erin McLellan is the author of several contemporary romances, all of which have characters who are complex, goodhearted, and a little quirky. She likes her stories to have a sexy spark and a happily ever after. Originally from Oklahoma, she currently lives in Alaska and spends her time dreaming up love stories set in the Great Plains. She is a lover of chocolate, college sports, antiquing, Dr Pepper, and binge-worthy TV shows.